WESTON

Sheppard's Shadow Book 4

KATHI S. BARTON

World Castle Publishing, LLC
Pensacola, Florida
Copyright © 2025 Kathi S. Barton
Hardback ISBN: 9798281993319
Paperback ISBN: 9798891263956
eBook ISBN: 9798891263963
First Edition World Castle Publishing, LLC, May 5, 2025
http://www.worldcastlepublishing.com
Licensing Notes
Cover: Cover Designs by Karen
Editor: Karen Fuller

Chapter 1

Rogen was putting the next sheet of sheetrock up on the wall when her sister, Belinda, contacted her. Being a cat made it easy for them to speak to each other like they were in the room together. Smiling before she even spoke, Rogen picked up the tape to fix the seams in the drywall before she moved on to the next wall to make sure it was set up well, too. As usual, her sister started out the conversation like they'd been talking all day long.

Belinda worked for a man near where she lived—the mayor of their little town, Weston Sheppard. He was paying her well, and she was happy. It was all she could do when she heard from her not to find the man and hug him for making her older sister as happy as she'd been of late. Rogen thought of all the people she knew, not counting that she was her sister, deserved this more. It was, she thought, just a bonus that she was making such good money on top of it all.

I have a clothing bonus as well as time paid for lunch, isn't that great? Not to mention the vacation I was telling you about last night. Two weeks is a nice one if you ask me. Especially when I've been here for such a short time period." She told her that was great as she lined up the last of the tape that would hold the wall together until the plaster dried. *"There's medical, too, but I don't know that I'll use that all that much with me being a cat and all. Today was proof that I might need to bring more clothing to work in case something happened and I had to shift."*

Pausing, she asked her what had happened there. Rogen felt better after hearing all the details about the men coming into the office to try and blackmail her boss about some playground equipment, but she still didn't care for the fact that she was literally in the line of fire with this job. She wouldn't tell her to quit working but decided that she was going to make sure her boss understood that if anything happened to Belinda, there would be a world of hurt brought down on him as the one who should be protecting her.

The room was finished by the time she was finished speaking to her sister. As she thought before, Belinda was happy. It had been a very long time since she'd heard her laughing and having a good time. When her husband had been killed a few years ago, all of them despaired of her ever recovering. Not only had Benson been killed, but their two children had been as well. It had been a fire in their home that had not just taken Belinda's family but everything in the house as well. Some items that she would never get back. And that hurt her to have no photos of her own with her kids in them.

"Whatcha up to?" Rogen looked up at her sister and partner, Sandy, and asked her how the other rooms were going. "I have two of the main rooms finished up, and they'll hopefully be painted tomorrow. That was a great idea that you had about the fans blowing directly on the walls. It's saved us about a week of getting this house finished. Not to mention the smell, too. It's easier to stand to be in the room when it doesn't smell like wet dog all the time."

"I spoke with the owner the other day, but I didn't mention that we'd be finished early. I believe that it would give the woman more things to think about changing in the house. I can't believe how much rework we've had to do because we told her that we had a day extra. No way am I telling her that we have a week. What's up with you now?" Sandy sat down on one of the large spools of wiring that had been being used for a table. "Is it that bad? What can I do for you? Slay some dragons? I will, you know."

"Danny wants me to quit working and stay at home more with him. I don't know how he expects money to be coming in when he doesn't have a job and me out of work as well. Just because you and I own the company doesn't mean that both of us didn't have to work." Sandy put up her hand to stop what Rogen knew was going to upset her. "I know. You told me not to marry him, but I was lonely. Not only that, but he was also working when I first met him. He's so different now. Just as you said, he'd be. Lazy and a jackass too."

"I don't think that he's any different but

just more vocal about it. He certainly is to me. What did you tell him about the partnership that the two of us have?" She didn't look at her but did tell Rogen that he knew that if she quit working, the company and everything else would go only to Rogen. That was the deal that they'd had made up when they went into business together. "I told you that was going to be the only thing that saved you. What did he have to say about that?"

"That he thinks you should have to buy me out so that he can—and he actually said so that he could have some extra money for the things that he does. The only thing that he does is spend money on those toys he's playing with." She finally looked up at her, and Rogen could see that she'd been crying. "Danny told me that I needed to get with child, and that would make you back off. Something about the two of us being too old to be working like we are and life passing us by. He's a moron. I don't know how he thinks that's going to happen. I've told him several times that I can't have his child, but he insists that I'm lying because you told me to. He acts like I can't have an opinion unless you give it to me. I'll say it again. He's a moron."

"Want me to have a talk with him?" Sandy told her that she didn't want to have to visit her in jail again. "That first time was all on him. It even came out in court that he drew his gun on me first. I wish more and more that I'd ended his life rather than spare it. I know that I'd sleep better at night."

"Don't kill him, please? He's not worth it. Especially for you ending up in jail or prison." Nodding, she noticed something on her sister that she'd not seen this morning when they were having breakfast to start the day. She moved her sister's hair out of the way and then started cursing. "I'm not even going to lie to you and say it was my fault. He backhanded me right before I left for work this morning because I didn't want him to go with the two of us to breakfast. All the two of you would do is fight and—where are you going?"

"I'm calling the family. Enough is enough." She waited for Sandy to tell her not to do it, to not involve the family, but when she picked up the phone, too angry to reach out to them, Sandy told her that Toby and Leanord would be working the fields and not hear her calling. That was all the okay that she needed to get Danny taken care of once and for all. The slimy bastard had hit the wrong person in hitting her sister.

After talking to all her brothers, she called Belinda later. She didn't want to upset her at work, and whatever they planned for the man wasn't going to include her sister. Belinda was fragile, and no one wanted her to be brought back down to where she was several years ago. Once she got her on the phone, it was only a matter of minutes before Belinda told her that not only was she going to help with Danny, she might well be the one that killed his fucking ass.

"I didn't think you'd want to be a part of it." She asked her why not, Sandy was her sister too. "She is, and I didn't mean to imply that she wasn't. But you've had a rough few years and are just now getting up on your feet. I didn't want to bring you down again. As far as I'm concerned, you're my sister as much as Sandy is."

"This is just what I need. To help her the

way that you all helped me. We all know that if not for your family, I wouldn't have survived. Just losing my husband was bad enough, but my...I lost everything, or so I thought. The rest of you wouldn't allow me to wallow in my self-pity, and I couldn't love you anymore for it." Rogen told her that she loved her. "And I love you too, Rogen, with all my being. But I want him out of her life, especially since he's knocking her around. Let me ask you something. Do you think it's the first time he's done it?"

"I didn't ask her. I don't think that I want to know." Belinda had to put her phone down to answer the door. She thought about hanging up, but when she heard the man's voice in the room with her sister, she did reach out to figure out if she was in trouble or not. Apparently, it was her boss coming by to tell her that he was going to go back into the office tonight so that he could take tomorrow off. Rogen thought that was nice of him.

"I might have to take some time off too. One of my sisters is being beaten up by the man that she's married to." He must have asked if he was a shifter because Belinda answered that. "No. Sandy was feeling lonely one night after coming to my house with the kids around her, and Danny came around, making her feel special. Then, about a week after they were married, he not only quit his job, but he started spending money that they didn't have. That's not true; they had the money, but it was not enough for him to spend it like he does all the time."

Rogen thought that she was telling the man a great deal about their soon to be ex brother-in-law, but she'd never met the man, nor did she trust easily. When her sister came back on the line, she started out with a plan to get Sandy away from Danny for a few days so that no one would blame her when he came up missing.

"And by that I mean dead." Rogen laughed, telling her sister that she'd never would have thought that she had that in her. "I'd like to think that I'm as strong as you are, but no one, not even our brothers, can outdo you. But I will help. And here's my plan."

After telling her that Sandy could come up there and talk to Weston, her boss, then she could stick around and help out his shadow when it came to training his people about construction and how to make it work. That was where Weston was going to be headed in the morning with his brothers Nash and Beau. After Sandy came there and worked for a while, then they could do whatever was necessary to get him out of her life.

"And what do you think your boss is going to say when he figures out that Sandy just happened to be around your boss when her husband of eleven years comes up missing? Someone might well miss the little fucker. Didn't you tell me that one of them was a shadow alpha?" She told her that was a brilliant idea. "Now, what have I said? I don't know if you realize this or not, but you talk a great deal in riddles. What did I have an idea about?"

"That they go there. Oh, this is great. Archie is a great man and a wonderful leader. I was actually thinking about joining this one here rather than have to pay part of my check to the one down there every week." Rogen asked her what she meant. "Since I've been here, I've been billed weekly a fine for not living with my shadow."

"He can't do that to you. At least, I'm reasonably sure that he can't. You told me, too, that you pledged to the leap leader there. Didn't you?" She said that she had but didn't have to pay any fees because she worked for his brother. "That's not right, honey. Let me look into things here, or you can talk with this Archie person and find out if that's true. How much is it that you've been paying?" She told her. "Holy Christ, Belinda, no wonder you were having so much trouble with keeping your lights on. That's about half of what you make, or close to it, I'm betting."

"Close. I guess I never thought that after all this time, I'd be cheated, so I just paid the fine and went on with my life. I wonder if, now that I have a better-paying job, he'll try and get more out of me?" Rogen told her to look into it and to make sure that she wasn't being told that she didn't have to pay the dues and then find out later that she did. "I have that in my paperwork. So I know that's true."

Rogen didn't know what to believe now.

As they were talking about the plans that she had, and it was a good one too, she decided that she was going to go and talk to their leader and find out about this. Then she thought that was a good way to get herself killed and decided to go to Belinda and find out from her boss. Since he wanted help, she was going to get as much from him as she could. No mother fucker was going to take advantage of her little family and get away with it. It just wasn't right.

She and Sandy finished up working on the house they were working on that evening. It was a big payday for them, but only if the woman who owned the house would quit changing her mind every three days. As it was now, they'd had to move the two outside doors over to make room for one more. Then there was the kitchen that had to have a bigger refrigerator as well as a six-burner stove that she could have her staff use. That had taken four more days of work just to get the kitchen looking like she wanted it. And she didn't want to get started thinking about how there was no carpet in the bedrooms four times then she wanted it back. The house had heated floors. Why did it need carpet anyway?

They'd not had it laid as yet, knowing that she was going to change her mind before things were wrapped up. Telling the woman that the carpet that she wanted, a bright white for the children's rooms, was on back order so that she'd not have to change it out again and again. Who put a white carpet in a kids' room in the first place? Rogen didn't have kids but knew better than that.

She was just glad that she didn't have to work outside with the woman. The lawn company had threatened to quit a dozen times, but the place still looked like a dump site for construction site debris. She was the house person, not, thankfully, the yard company.

Even the thought of having a white carpet in a kid's room gave her the willies. Toby had four kids of his own, and each one of them could tear up anything white in a matter of minutes and not even get themselves dirty in the process.

She was home packing up when she heard back from her sister. The entire Sheppard family was coming to them to talk about business and to meet their leader, too. Rogen wasn't sure about that and told her sister that but it was a done deal. They were coming and were going to help take care of Danny, the shithead. She wanted to knock the shit out of him now, but she would wait on the bigger team coming. If they fucked up, she'd find a place to bury them as well. All of them.

~*~

Weston looked over the paperwork again and had to sigh. It wasn't written in the bylaws of their kind, so how the hell was Franklin getting away with basically double charging for fees and dues when a person worked in another shadow, not to mention had pledged to the other shadow in the first place? It made no sense at all to him. Apparently, to Archie, either. And he was a shadow leader.

"I can't find where it's in his laws either. And I'm not sure that he could do it in the first place, as she is a part of my group." Archie handed him the book that they'd unearthed from the previous leap leader's office before tearing down the building. "According to the laws made by the king, the only one that can be charged for living outside of a leap is the leader if he's in another territory without permission. And I can't think of a single reason that should be happening. Can you?"

"No. Not unless it's for something like what is going on now. And even that, it's no reason to charge someone simply for getting answers about a job." The Watson family was going to come up here and train a few of their pack on how to lay sheetrock. In the past month, not only had they gotten some younger people in the shadow, but they were willing to learn a new trade to be able to help with the construction of a couple of new businesses that were coming to town, too. "You don't have to do anything either to get them to come here other than to make sure that they're paid a reasonable wage. And it's up to you if you want to charge them or not any fees."

"We're going to make sure they have a place to stay while here too. It's the least we can do for their helping us out." Weston asked him where they were staying. "We have some homes around town they can stay in while here. The women are the ones that are going to be helping out. Their brothers are coming for a little time off since it's the end of the season for them."

He thought about what Belinda had told him about Sandy's spouse and wondered if he should mention it as well, so he decided against it. Danny would show himself while here, and that would be the end of him. Weston might well do it himself. He didn't think men or women should beat up on one another. It was bad enough when they did it to their kids.

By the time he was ready to go home, he was exhausted. Mentally, all he wanted to do was to turn off his head, but his body, too, from helping move some of the filing cabinets around in his office, was hurting him as well.

By the time he finished up his dinner, he was sitting on the couch and watching the news. There wasn't too much more he could take today, so by ten, he was in bed and about asleep. It was then that his brother Beau decided to contact him. He'd never turn down an opportunity to talk to one of his family members, but today had been a shitty one, and he just wanted to sleep.

"I won't keep you long. I just have a couple of questions you might have an answer to." He told him to ask him. *"Calhoun is the brother that is going to work with the town on the advertising that we need, correct? If so, then I'm not sure what it is that I can do to help him. He's really talented. You should see his work."*

"From my understanding, he's only going to help out with the adverts that are to bring in more businesses. I guess Sunny and Carrie have a list of the ones that have contacted them. Amber has the workup on them so that we can hit all their selling points to get them here." He asked him how that worked if they were already coming here. *"I don't know, Beau. I only know that we have to have some kind of billing and a list of things on this thing to get them here. Just because they say they want to put in a business doesn't mean all that much if they don't know what their perks will be."*

"Good point. All right. It was something that just occurred to me." He was dozing off when his brother spoke again. *"What if one of them, the sisters, I mean, is my mate? Or yours? What if she's*

the married one? And I end up killing her husband or something."

"We've been told that he's not her mate, so it'll not matter, I guess. We'll just have to cross that when it comes to it, I guess." He thought about what his brother said about being mates. *"I suppose we might any of us be mates to them. But I'm not going to stress about it unless I have to."*

"You're right. I shouldn't either. My house is being built, and if it comes to that, I can have the faeries finish it up if I need it quicker. I might do that anyway, just to get it out of the way." He told his brother that he was tired and in bed. *"Right. I'll talk to you in the morning. Sorry to have bothered you, Weston, I needed to talk to you."*

"Anytime, little brother. We can have breakfast in town if you want." After making arrangements, he closed his eyes and decided to try to will himself to sleep.

When that didn't work, he got up and decided to have his house out of the way as well. Faeries didn't sleep, so he was all right with getting them going. The only thing that he'd wanted was the option to change things up if his mate didn't like it. They were more than happy to do that for him.

It only took them a few minutes to finish up the house. His bedroom wasn't the master suite, and he was all right that they'd made it up to be neutral for his mate if he ever got one. As it was now, he was thinking along the lines of finding someone who wanted to go out and have a good time, knowing that it wasn't going to go any further than that. He was happy to be dating in his leap, where no one cared about commitment.

By the time it was time for him to meet his brother, Weston decided to get dressed up. He was not in a suit, but he did wear a tie with his jeans. It felt right to be looking better than just a pair of jeans and a tee shirt for a change.

The restaurant wasn't all that busy, so he was seated right away. Looking over the menu while waiting, he decided to have the endless biscuits and gravy. They served it with fresh coffee or tea, and he could get up to three sides if he wanted. Of course, he got all three sides of the hashbrown casserole with orange juice and fresh sliced tomatoes for his salad.

When Beau showed up with Nash and the others, he was thrilled beyond words. All six of them could put a dent in some biscuits and gravy, but he was overjoyed to be able to talk to them. His day was starting out much better than he could have imagined.

No business was discussed, but they did check their phones when they went off. If it had been scheduled, this time with them, none of them would even have done that. But they were busy men with a great deal going on at all times.

Archie was the busiest of the six of them. He had taken over their leap, but they also knew that his mate, Carrie, was getting close to her due date, and they all wanted to be there for the next generation to come to the family. There was Wills in the family, but he was the oldest kid he knew at ten. It would be fun to have not just little ones in the family but perhaps little girls around, too. They were keeping it secret as to what Carrie was carrying right now.

They'd only had to wait on food once, and it wasn't so bad. The biscuits were fresh, as were the potatoes they got. He also knew that they'd all tip well and also slip some money to the kitchen staff for helping them out. Apparently, Archie had called ahead to let them know they were all coming in for the special this morning. He loved that they liked to do things locally.

The meeting with the Watson family was going to be on time, and he seriously thought about going into his office just to take a nap. Being up for over twenty-four hours was more than he thought he might be able to handle what with all the carbs he'd had for breakfast, too. Just as he was going into his office and closing the door, a man showed up, saying that he was there to go over the perks they were going to give him for allowing his wife to work with his leap.

"You must be Danny." He asked how he'd known that, seemingly very proud of the fact that he'd heard of him. "No, not in any way that you're thinking. I just knew that one of the sisters is married to a human that isn't her mate."

"Yeah, my wife, Sandy. Rogen is her sister, and she's a real ball-buster if you ask me." He didn't but didn't comment. "We're trying for a baby right now. Well, I guess I'm going to have her see the doctor soon. She must not be as fertile as the rest of them are. One of them brothers has seven kids or something like that."

"Four. They have four, and it's doubtful that there is anything wrong with Sandy other than you're not her mate. But that's not why you're here, is it? You mentioned perks. What were you thinking? And just so you know, there won't be any monetary perks unless you're working too." He said that wasn't fair as the job was keeping him from his wife. "And? That has nothing to do with us. We're already putting the family up with housing and staff if necessary. Sandy is working for us and making a good wage. Whatever else you need isn't anything we're going to worry with."

"Maybe she won't work then? You might not understand this being single, but she does what I tell her so that she doesn't get knocked around." All he did was stand up so that he could see the fear on the other man's face. "I was just joking. God damn it, it was a joke."

"It's time you left." Nodding, the other

man stood up. "And there will be no bothering Sandy when she's working for my brother either. She's here to do a job, and unless, as I said, you're working too, then you'll stay out of the way."

He left five minutes later after telling him again that it had all been a joke. It wasn't that he wasn't in the mood for a good joke, but the man had hit his wife, and all jokes weren't funny to him.

By the time he headed to the meeting place, leaving Belinda in charge of the office, he had a list of questions for his older brother about her having to pay leap fines while working for him. He'd not realized that wasn't a rule until he looked into it. Sitting at the long conference table, he was happy to see that Danny wasn't there. The rest of the family was, so he asked Archie his questions so that they could all get answers about what was going on.

"I did look it up in the by-laws, and there isn't a law that says that she has to pay the fines. I've contacted our king, Major Ramit. His first name is Major, not a rank. He said that he's had trouble with that shadow before. He is going to look into other things that he's heard. Also, none of this will get back to your leader, as he said he's been hearing complaints about him before." Leanord asked if she'd get a refund. "If she doesn't get one from her previous leap, she will get one from mine. I'll make it right for her."

"Thank you for that." Archie looked at him when the man had a second question. "We, my brothers have come here on our own to be able to hang out with Belinda. We miss her, and I know that the kids do as well. I want to personally thank you for allowing us all to be here, too."

"We were hoping that you could help with some of your skills as well. We could use some ideas on how to get a garden going. We were thinking something like a community garden where the people who want can have their own place to get veggies and such." Toby, the man with four kids, said that there were plenty of benefits to having a garden started now. "Good, that's what we were hoping for. A way to make sure that we can get what we need going by the time summer comes around."

The meeting lasted for several hours. He

was having too much fun to be exhausted and was glad that Archie told them that dinner would be at his house tonight. They were all happy about that, and he was looking forward to being able to talk to them all about the suggestions that they'd brought up in dealing with a new company. It would bring in another fifty jobs by summer if things went the way that he wanted.

Chapter 2

Major didn't care for the little man in front of him. But so far, he'd not made any moves so that he could kill him. And he wanted to, in the worst sort of way, just to get him away from him. The man was a shyster, as his mother would have said, and he needed to be eliminated sooner rather than later.

"They have the money. I don't see why it would bother you if they're running a little short. I mean, it all goes to someplace in the leap." Another thing that he didn't like about the man was that while he wasn't telling him everything, he was just short of telling the truth, too, like what he just said. It was only benefiting him, the people paying dues, and since he was in the leap as well, he was getting the extra cash. "Is this about that Warrior family? They bitch about everything anymore. From having to pay monthly fines to having to go outside the leap for jobs. Some people just aren't happy unless they're complaining all the time. Or is it the Watsons? They're getting on my last nerve about everything as well."

"That's another thing that I wanted to talk to you about. Once someone pledges to another leader, you can't charge them for fees in your own. You should be bringing in more jobs if you need to have income coming from people that no longer want to be a part of what you're doing here." He said the name Belinda Watson. "I don't know her. But if she's the first person that pops into your head about what I just said, then don't do it anymore. If you wanted her to stay in your leap, then you'd have to go another way, like having more jobs for the people here. This isn't working the way that it's supposed to be. It's for the others, not just to benefit you."

"She's not told me directly that she's going to another leap." He asked him why he'd say it that way. "Well, I was notified that she was thinking about pledging to someone named Sheppard, but she has to tell me herself before I believe it."

"It's a done deal for her if she's talking about Archie Sheppard. Now, there is a good leader. You should go and talk to him about having things done for the betterment of the leap. You could learn a few things." And if he ended up dead there, it would be all the better for him. "In fact, you're to go to him in the coming weeks to get information from him. I'm telling you this directly to your face and reminding you again that what I say goes. If you're charging this Belinda person for fines, get together what she's paid you and return it to her. Without more fees or penalties, too. She's in a different leap, and that's all there is to it."

"That's a bit of money I've collected from her. How about I just say that she's off the hook for now and tell her that she's fine. For now." Major stood up and put both hands on the desk of the man in front of him. It was the most intimidating stare he had, and it didn't take long for the man to pull out his checkbook and start writing out a check. Major told him cash and he'd made sure she got it. "It's going to hurt me if I have to pay that back to her now. I have investments that need to be paid from that."

"Cash. Now." When he opened the drawer that was to his left, Major got a good look at the amount of cash that was just lying there. Instead of commenting on it, he pulled out the biggest stack of more money than he'd seen in one place before. "Is this from you charging fines from people no longer in your leap?"

"Yes. It does add up." The large ledger was next. "Let's see how much she's paid in fines and dues?"

It totaled to be more than ten grand, and Major was embarrassed that he thought it might work for him, too. But only for a second. The ten thousand dollars hardly made a dent in the money in the drawer, which had him grabbing the ledger from the man to see what else he was going to be dealing with.

He had to sit down hard when he realized that families were paying for their family members to be buried on the land that was set up for them. Then, there were taxes on things like going to school on the land. Car taxes, as well as baby taxes. A family of six was paying out sixteen percent—four percent per child of their income to have children. No wonder people weren't pledging to the leap here. They would go broke if they hung out longer than a couple of kids in their family.

"You're fired. I can't have you doing this to others who depend on their leap to be there for them, and you're gouging them all the time." He had him remove all the money from the drawer and count it. "There is fifty-eight thousand dollars here, you idiot. Why don't you have it in a bank or something so that you can—Christ. You're using this money as your own cash, aren't you?"

"I have expenses, too, you know. I mean, I get paid from the accounts, but this is better for me all the way around. This way, I don't have to use my own money for things that I can just get. You have no idea how much little things can catch up with you when you don't have cash just lying around. I bet that I save myself fifty grand a week by just having cash around."

"The only reason you have it around is because you're stealing it from the members of your own leap." He just smiled at him. "I was right in firing you. I should use you as an example of what happens to people who take advantage of people they're supposed to be caring for. But I'm afraid it'll get around to how you're doing this, and others will think that they can do it."

"Thank you." Major growled and started putting money in a bank bag that was also in the drawer. He had to wonder if there was more money around that had been stolen but didn't want to think about it. "To think that you want to brag on me and what I do around here makes me feel special."

There was no help for it. He was going to have to kill the man so that word didn't get around on what he'd been doing so that others were stealing from the very hand that paid them. As it was now, there were going to be people coming out of the woodwork on trying to figure out how things had gotten so out of hand like this had.

Having Franklin arrested was the least of his problems. He might well lose his own job from this. After spending nearly six hours going over the ledger—the man had kept good books as to where the money was coming from—he had a small accounting of what Franklin's leap was owed. As it was now, he was going to have to spend weeks hunting down others who had been cheated and were no longer a part of this shadow. Christ, he was going to need help and decided to call up Archie Sheppard. The man would know just how to get things going to make this right.

After telling him what had happened, the man didn't say anything for some time. He didn't want to think that he might well have hung up on him. It would have been something he might have been tempted to do. Just as he was going to say his name, Archie spoke again.

"I'm thinking that this isn't a single-month deal. I know that Belinda has been paying out the ass since moving here three years ago." Major said he didn't know how long it had been going on. "I see."

"I don't blame you for thinking that I should have been more up on things. I have been feeling that I've failed the people here myself.

I've actually thought about stepping down from being king with this plot." Archie asked him if he'd really do that. "I have been thinking on it hard, I must admit. What would you do had you been in my position? You're a good man, Archie, and if you think that I should step down, then I will."

"Someone else would just take over that would think it was all right with the way things have been going. No, you're in a position to fix this, and that's what needs to be done." He didn't care for his answer and told him so. "I don't know what to tell you. Since I've been a leap leader, all you've done is tell me to fix this when you have your own mess to clean up after. No, I'm in no position to tell you what to do. I'm grateful that I don't have anything going on here that might cause me to quit what I'm doing."

Major had known that Archie was an honest man. He'd not thought that he'd be so honest with him. But he didn't want to go get into who was to blame, so he decided to make things right. And he would. Not living up to someone's expectations was a painful pill to swallow, especially when it came from such a good man as he knew Archie to be.

They spoke about giving the money back, and Archie explained to him that might not be the way to go. People would be coming to him for more money than he might have, and that wasn't going to be helping anyone. So, for his help, it was decided to give the money back to Belinda because, without her help, it would never have come up. He was also going to use the money found for projects that poorer shadows might need help with, like new schools and better homes for the elderly.

After another hour of talking to the younger man, he had a better outlook on the way things were going. There was something so wonderful about having fresh eyes on things that he was glad now that he'd spoken to him. Archie was going to be taking his job when he retired or, for that matter fucked up again, and Major knew that he'd do a great job. Much better than he thought he'd done since taking over the position from his own father.

Major spent the rest of the afternoon and

well into the evening going over books. They'd been right, or Archie had been in saying that this thing with Franklin had been an ongoing thing. As soon as he was ready to call it quits for the day, he'd found the account for Franklin that had several hundred thousand dollars in it, as well as the ledgers on where the money had come from.

Needing to have a good run, he decided that he was going to disband Franklin's leap. There were only twenty-four people in the leap, six of which was Franklin's family. Almost as soon as he made it known about the leap, he heard from four of the families asking to go to Archies. Giving them the permission to do so had him thinking that in the next few weeks, the same thing would be happening to the rest of the people. Good for them both was all he could think about.

Getting home that night, he told his mate what he'd found. He knew that she would not say anything to anyone about how he'd taken the advice of Archie but she did point out that Archie might well be better at his job than any other leader he had. She didn't even cut him any slack when she said he'd be better than him about it as well. It hurt to his core, but she was right. There was a good chance that not only would Archie make a better king, but he'd be a better person for the job all the way around, too.

That night, when he went to bed, he felt the guilt of what had happened right under his nose. He should have paid more attention when people were complaining about Franklin and looked into it. Major knew that Archie would have. Looking out his window as he was closing his curtains, he decided that he was going to groom Archie for his position if it was the las thing he did. A better man needed to be in his place, and soon.

Getting up the next morning, Major was feeling better about his job. He'd not do the things that he'd thought of in the darkness of the night, but he would be a better king. Starting today, he was going to start visiting other leaps if for no reason than it was necessary for his own peace of mind. That alone made him feel like he was doing the right things, things that he should have been doing all along.

It took him until that evening to come to an understanding of himself. He had been lax in his job, and doing something about it made him feel better. Now that he had a plan, a good one, he thought, Major even felt better about his thoughts on the money. He'd use it for good. His ideas of using it for all leaps had him making notes even as he was readying himself for bed that evening. Yes, he thought to himself. He was going to be a king that Archie could be proud of.

~*~

Belinda was excited to have her money returned to her. She didn't even mind that it was all in cash. It was easier to use but harder to explain. But use it, she did. The first thing she did was to put a downpayment on her own home. She'd been living in a small apartment since moving to the little town, and it was too much for her. Getting herself a little home with two bedrooms felt right. Also, she had enough of a yard that she would have herself a garden come spring. Something that she had missed since her family had been killed.

Walking home from work, she saw Danny,

Sandy's soon-to-be ex-husband, coming out of the local store with several bags of something. Standing in front of him when he stopped at a curb, she asked him what he was doing.

"Not that it's any of your business, but I'm buying myself a treat. I've been stuck in that crummy house for two days, and I need something to do." She told him to get a job. "I will not. I have a wife who works, and that's going to change soon enough, too. Sandy is going to have my baby soon, and we'll be living in the high life with the money that we get from Rogen when she buys out our part in the business."

"She is not going to have your baby. You've been told several times that you're not her mate and she won't have your baby." He told her that was an old wives tale. "No, it's the truth. As for the business, Rogen won't have to buy her out because they're partners, splitting everything down the middle. If Sandy leaves, then all the business will go to Rogen. It's in their contract that they split everything down the middle, including costs and pay."

"I'm getting me an attorney." She told him

good luck with that. "You're always so mean to me. What did I ever do to you that has you hating me so much?"

"Several things come to mind. One of them being that you're a lazy fuck. Where do you get off spending Sandy's hard-earned money when she's trying to make ends meet?" He told her his opinion on that. "So you set up a charge at the store in the name of the Sheppards? You can't do that, you idiot. I'm going to take care of that right now."

She saw Weston coming toward her and told him what was going on. Making Danny turn over the bags while standing there, she went with Weston to take the things back to the store. He made it known that the Sheppards weren't going to be footing the cost for anything that wasn't business-related for the Watsons nor, as it turned out, for the Martins either. Weston didn't find it funny, but she did when Weston tried to explain to Danny about children as well. The man was a moron, just as she'd been told about him since he married Sandy.

"What do you say about firing Sandy so

that the two of us can hang around here in the house while the others work?" Weston asked him why he'd do that. "Because I'm bored, and since you hired us to make some business in your town, the least you could do is pick up the tab while I'm here."

"No." She nearly burst out laughing when Weston told him no. The man was good at it, too. He never felt the need to explain why he didn't want to do whatever it was, but just simply said he wasn't going to do it no matter what he said. "Not that you'll have any luck from now on but don't be charging things to accounts your ass isn't able to cover. And so you're aware, if, for any reason, Sandy quits, she'll be out of a house and income. I read over the contracts like you should have done. No work means no pay."

Belinda met up with her family later that afternoon. Telling them what had happened about Danny had them all laughing, including Sandy. She felt sorry for her sister-in-law. Being in a loveless marriage was hard on people. As soon as she left to go back to her own home, her new home, Belinda began knitting her first blanket in a very long time.

By the time she was ready for bed, she'd gotten nearly fifty rows finished and a start on the pretty little baby's blanket that she decided to do for Wrangler and his wife. While she didn't know the sex of the baby, the first scents of her being with child had her wishing for her own family again.

Benson had been a good man and a great father. They'd met when she'd been barely a baby and him being ten years old. Knowing that they were mates their entire lives had made them not just husband and wife but best friends as well. When their first child had been born, Benny, she thought that the world was the best place a person could have been. Then Sarah had come along, and life was suddenly perfect for the four of them.

After five years, they decided to have another child. She'd been out with her own family, her parents dying not long after her own family for her father's birthday. The kids who had been playing in their pool all evening were too exhausted to go with her so Benson had stayed home with them. He had thought to make things romantic for the two of them and had lit candles all over their bedroom that night.

She'd been gone all evening, having only to come home to a fully engulfed home and her family gone. It still, to this day, broke her to think about it. If only she'd made them come with her, they might well all be alive. When her phone rang, she nearly didn't answer it.

"I can feel your pain." Bursting into tears, she spoke to Rogen when she answered. Telling her that it wasn't as bad as the first few months but that there were times when she just couldn't function. Like tonight. "I'm so sorry you hurt. When I think about my big brother being gone, I can't help but think about Benny or Sarah, either. I'm so sorry, honey."

They talked for hours, and it wasn't until Rogen told her that she was nearly to her house that she remembered that she'd been finishing the house they'd been working on before leaving there. The house was finished now, and all the things that went into building a new house were completed before they could leave. Rogen was going to be staying with her for the duration of the contract to help the other leap, and she couldn't have been happier. At midnight, the two of them were crying in their popcorn, talking about all the things that had happened since the death of her brother and Belinda's family.

"Once, when Benson was younger, before you two got married, he told me that he was going to have himself a bachelor pad and never come out of it to date anyone. Mom thought that he was insane and had that look on her face like she didn't believe it either. Being the oldest, Benson had this weird code of conduct that the rest of us would laugh at all the time. He actually used to tell me that he was going to go on each of my dates to scare men away. Like I date all that much now." She told her that she should be dating. "No thanks. In my line of work, I see all kinds of human couples and their stupid fights. It would just like the fates to give me a human mate so that he'd turn out to be just like Danny."

"Danny was never the right person for Sandy. Even before they started dating, I could see what an ass he was." Rogen said that she'd forgotten that she'd known the other man. "Yes. We were in some classes together in high school. Even then, he was forever trying to get out of work by being sly."

"We all tried to warn her, but it's going to work out fine in the end. He'll be stupid enough that someone will have to kill his ass, then he'll be gone." She told her about the game system that he'd tried to charge to the Sheppard's account. "You know, that doesn't surprise me in the least bit. He would think that it was all right that he'd be able to do something like that."

After a time, it was bedtime for her as she had to work in the morning. Rogen said that she had a meeting with Archie in the morning about some things that had come up in the local pack and was having her usual breakfast with Sandy, too.

"You should join us. It'll be fun to have you around." She said that Weston was going to be at the meeting too and that she needed to open the offices. "I forgot about you working again. I'm glad you are."

She didn't mention the extra money that

she had that would have made it so that she'd not have to work so hard as she'd been asked not to do. But when Rogen hugged her, telling her that if she needed any extra money to let her know, she told her what was going on.

"That's wonderful. I'll take that off my list of things to talk to Archie about when I see him. I was going to be a bitch about it, so thanks for letting me know." Belinda told her how she'd purchased the house with the extra income and was going to be saving a great deal of money by not having to pay for the extra fines. "They're not going to be charging us for staying here either. Not to mention providing housing for us. I heard that Toby and Rachel are having a wonderful time while here with the kids."

"Toby and Lenord are also helping with the construction training. I didn't remember until then that you'd all been in the construction business that your parents left you guys." Rogen told her that it had been in the family for a couple of generations before they'd taken it over. "Lenord said that he missed it but didn't. He loved the physical part of it but didn't care for being indoors all the time. I think that Toby loves being inside, but not the physical part. He's more of a farmer who drives the tractor, though they both make it work for themselves. And a nice income as well."

As she was getting ready for bed later, she thought about Weston and her family. He treated her well, and she wished they lived closer to her now. Weston and his family were so close that she couldn't imagine thinking about one of them without the others. They were that tight of a family. She supposed it had a lot to do with their mother and grandfather, but she didn't ask. She loved having enough of them around so as not to miss her own family at times.

Belinda usually didn't sleep well in a new bed. But since she'd been living in her own home with her own things around her, she'd been sleeping better. Having Rogen in the house helped as well. She was someone that she could rely on, more so than her own brother and sister, and she would have gone to the ends of the earth for any of the Watsons. More so with Rogen.

Rogen was hard on people. She didn't hold

back on things when she needed to say them. That was something that she'd enjoyed...well, not enjoyed but valued about her after Benson had been killed. She'd been up in her face daily when she thought that she'd been feeling sorry for herself long enough. She'd been right in saying it, too. Belinda knew that the only reason that she was a functioning person was because of Rogen. And she'd never forget that.

When she got up the next morning, Rogen had left to go on a run. That was another thing that she'd forgotten about her was that when she wasn't working, Rogen ran. It kept her in shape and satisfied her cat when she couldn't get in a full day on the job.

By the time she'd gotten to the office and opened up, she had four messages for Weston and two for his brother. While Archie was setting up his own office, she suggested that he had his calls forwarded to her so that she could help him out. The man had been so grateful that he'd gotten her a dozen red roses and a box of chocolates as his way of saying thanks. She enjoyed it as it was teaching her some more about the cats that she worked with and had as family.

By noon, when she'd not heard from anyone, she closed up and made her way to the diner to get some lunch. She had been eating at her desk, but Weston had nipped that. He said that she needed downtime as much as anyone did and for her to leave in the middle of something if she had to just to eat. So that was what she was doing when Wills, son of Wrangler, joined her. He was such a wonderful little boy that she decided that he'd make a good companion for lunch.

"Dad gave me money. He said that since I'm working at the pack house that I need to be paid for lunch. I'm helping them pack up the main house so that it can be torn down for a better place." He snapped his fingers. "Pack house. That's what it's called. They have all kinds of books in the place about their kind. I asked Uncle Archie, and he told me that he was still finding things in the leap house before they did the same and started on something new."

They had an enjoyable lunch, and he walked her back to the mayor's office. Weston was there but locked up in his offices, so she didn't bother him. It wasn't until Rogen came in that she found out that the meeting hadn't gone as well as they had hoped because she was mated to Weston.

"You're kidding." She didn't look any too pleased about being a mate any more than she'd been for paying double fines. "Weston is a great catch. You remember me telling you about him, don't you?"

"He's not happy either." She didn't understand that either, as she thought Weston was a great guy. "Yeah, to you. I'm going to have to uproot my entire life just because I'm mated to him. I just got things where I want them."

"Did he say that to you? Tell you that you were going to have to do that?" It didn't sound like him, so she was glad when Rogen told her that he'd not. "Good. You should talk to him before jumping to conclusions, Rogen. It's not like you to do that either."

Leaving at five o'clock, Weston still did not come out of his office. She thought that she'd give him one more day before she started pounding on his door. It wasn't going to change things, the two of them being at odds, but she wasn't going to allow either of them to not bask in the idea of being mates either. Idiots.

Chapter 3

"Where are you?" Weston told his brother that he was in his office. "I've heard that you're not coming out. What is the big deal? So what, you've met your mate. Come out and enjoy her."

"I'm not avoiding her." Archie asked him what he was doing then. "I'm getting work done so that when she's ready to leave, I can go with her. She and her family have a life that's not here. I want to be able to leave here and this office in good shape so that things get done. You should see how much I've gotten done."

He'd not gotten all that done if he was honest with himself. He'd find himself distracted by the smallest things. The sun shining, and he'd wonder if she was enjoying it. The phone ringing—which it did a great deal would have him sitting on pins and needles, wondering if she needed him.

Weston didn't think that there would ever

be a time when she needed him, but he could hope. She was the most capable woman he'd ever met. Asking his brother what he wanted, he saw that there were only two more files that needed his attention before he had to go out and find Belinda again to figure out what else he had to do.

After the first couple of days of him working nonstop in his office, she came in and yelled at him. She scolded him like a child about being immature about having a mate until he told her what he was doing. He could tell that she was pissed off at him, but thankfully, she was able to see what he'd been up to as well. Twenty-three projects were just waiting on approval for them to get started, and he'd have most of the school projects finished up—or at least started before he left for Tennessee for his new life. In the last three days, he'd been focusing all his energy on getting himself in a good place so that he'd be able to leave his family, too.

"Do you have time to go over the contracts for the school board that give you the okay to hire someone to come in and repaint all the walls?"

He knew that the school needed a whole new overhaul, but without the funding right now, they had to work with what they had. "Also, I have the okay to purchase new computers for the library. Twenty of them to start and more as the money comes in."

"Why are they going to the library and not the classrooms?" Weston explained to his brother about the internet not being in the classrooms as yet. "That sounds like a problem that needs to be taken care of first."

"I agree, but without the funding, then it's not going to happen. As it stands right now, if we were to tear out the walls to put in the internet in the school, then we'd run into more problems that would be more costly. With everything being tied up with the cash, then nothing is going to happen." Archie started cursing. "I couldn't agree more, but until the funds are released, if ever, there just isn't enough money in the budget to even have the lots plowed this winter without going in the red."

It wasn't right that the money was there; it had been found in some offshore accounts from the time that Mayor Hathaway was in office, and they couldn't use it. The feds were hoping that they'd get it back to their little town in the next five years. Five years was a long time to wait and see if you ever got the money that had been earmarked for so many different projects that hadn't been done. It was like you could see at the end of the tunnel, yet there wasn't any movement coming at the end of it.

After talking to his brother about other projects that were going on that needed money, he was disappointed when he told him that they'd have to figure out something so that the town could have some improvements. The only way he could see that was if more businesses were coming in to help out with employment or if they were to raise taxes again in a town that had been down on its luck for some time now. Even the sidewalks needed some improvements before someone was seriously hurt.

He was just headed to lunch when Rogen showed up. She looked pissed off, and he felt his cat curl around him a little tighter. She sat down—really, she flopped down in the chair across from him and asked him what the fuckery he was doing.

"Working. Same as you." She told him the same thing that Belinda had. He was hiding out. He explained what he was doing much in the same way as he'd done his brother. That he was working so that he'd be ready to go when she was. "You're not staying here, are you?"

"What do you mean? I'm not leaving until the training is done." He told her that was all he was doing, and she looked confused. "I thought you'd order me to stay here with you as your family is here."

"First of all, I'd never order you to do anything. This will work only if we work together, and I'm willing to do that. Secondly, your family isn't here but there and I thought you'd want to be closer to them. I know that they're all here now, but it couldn't be much longer before you're finished here and want to return home." She nodded and stared at him. "I more than likely look like I'm hiding from you, but I'm trying my best to finish a job up, same as you would, so that I can go with you when you're ready to leave. I will admit that I was hiding from you, but that's only because I was trying my best not to piss you off by annoying you. You seemed to get annoyed easily of late."

"I thought you were going to demand things of me that I didn't want to do." He asked her if she'd met the other women in his family. "I have, but they didn't seem to have any family that they wanted to spend some time with, so they stayed. I'm sorry if it sounds like I was... well, I was being a bitch, but I didn't understand why you were avoiding me."

"As I said, I have been avoiding you on some level. I didn't want to be a pest. But being holed up in this office is making it so that things can be finished up after I leave, which will benefit the town. I'm hoping to leave it in better shape than when I arrived." She asked him about the position he was in as mayor. "I'm no longer thinking of running. I want to make a life wherever you are for as long as I can. And make you happy too."

"I'm rarely happy anymore." She went on to explain about Danny and her sister/

partner. How he was making things difficult for everyone that was around, too. He told her about the gaming system that he had charged to the family. "See? Right there is why I can't be happy. He's already embarrassed us several times since we've been here, and it has nothing to do with him just being a lazy fuck but more with him being a fucking bastard. He's hitting around my sister too. Twice since we've been here. Sandy isn't going to be able to come back home with him if this keeps up. You're going to find his body alongside of the road soon, and either myself or one of the other family members — including Belinda are going to end up in jail or, worse yet, prison because we're going to knock him around until he's dead."

He couldn't help it, he laughed. She grinned, too, and Weston fell a bit more in love with his beautiful little mate. Rogen was everything that he'd ever hoped for in a mate and more. But that didn't mean that he wasn't slightly afraid of her, too. She was strong and smart, too.

Inviting her to have lunch with them, he

and Belinda had lunch daily to go over messages and files that she was working on with him, Rogen agreed. It wasn't until they were eating that he realized that she had been eating at the same sub place he had daily. They even ate the same kind of double meat sub and enjoyed it with pretzels, not chips.

The rest of the day had him still locked up in his office, but he was getting more done now that he wasn't trying to hide away. He still did, but not so much from his mate and family. By the time it was five o'clock, he was ready to go home. It was hard work knowing that a lot of the town depended on him to get things finished up even though there was no money to be had. Not even to pay his salary.

He was shocked to see a moving van in front of his house. There was a man sitting on the front porch that looked familiar. In addition to the moving van, there were several pieces of luggage there as well. He asked the man who he was and what he was doing.

"You got my father kicked out of his job." He asked him who that would be. "My dad was

the mayor, and you got him fired. I don't enjoy
the life that is going on with them now, so I've
come here to live with you. You'll have to give
me a key. Sitting out here in the sun isn't any
way that you should be treating me."

"What do you mean, I need to give you a
key? To what?" He told him a key to his house
and then called him stupid for not getting that.
"I'm not going to give you a key to my house.
You don't live here."

"Not yet, thanks to you locking me out.
I'll expect you to give me the best rooms, it's
the least you can do for making me wait all this
time. And I'll need for you to put it out there
that you're responsible for my well-being. A
credit card would be nice, but if you just tell all
the merchants around town that you're going to
be footing my bills, it'll be the same thing." He
asked his name. "Yes, you would need that for
the line of credit you're going to be giving me.
Hank Hathaway. And don't be putting a limit
on things for me. I've gotten used to the finer
things in life, and I'm not going to be giving that
up because you took my dad's job. There will

be a few in Columbus as well, but we'll get to those." He eyed him. "Well? Aren't you going to be opening the door anytime soon?"

"Not for you. I don't understand what's going on here. You think that you're going to be moving into my home and charging up credit in my name around town? That's not going to happen. Nor are you moving in with me." Hank told him that he'd have to, as he had nowhere else to go. "Like I care. You're not going to get anything from me. I took over the job because your father was a liar and a cheat."

"Yes, well, I don't know about all that. I do know that you're responsible for his losing his job and thus my income, so you're going to take over for him until such a time as my dad has his job back. Until then, I'm sure you can understand that you need to make sure that I'm cared for in the manner I'm accustomed to so that I don't lose out on the finer things of life. It's the least you can do for what you've done to me."

"No, the least I can do is have you arrested for trespassing. You're not moving in here." Hank stared at him as if he wasn't understanding why he wasn't doing what he wanted. "Is this moving van yours? Get it off my property, too."

"The moving van is for you. You have to move out so that I can move in. Listen, I don't understand why you're having so much trouble with this. You got my income cut off by having my father fired, and because of that, you have to step up and take care of me. I'll require a staff too. This is a big house, and I can't be responsible for cooking and cleaning up after myself." He sat down on the bench that the faeries had put in for him to use. "I'm calling the police. This is just stupid on your part to think that I'm going to have anything to do with your living arrangements." Before he could get the first number dialed, his phone was knocked from his hand and flew across the yard. He asked him what he was doing.

"You're starting to piss me off. I've explained this to you several times, and that's just the way things are going to go. You'll move your things out of this house and allow me to live in here at no cost. You owe me." He told him that he didn't owe him anything. "Now listen here.

I've been nice until now, and if you don't open that door and start moving your things out of my way, I'm going to really get angry, and you'll not like that. This is what is going to happen, so you might as well get on board with it from the start, and things will go easier for you."

"*I have a problem here. And I need someone to call the police.*" After reaching out to his family and explaining what was going on, it was Jameson that said he'd call the police, and since he was nearly to his house, he'd be there for him. "*He's saying that since I got his father fired that I need to take over his care. The man has to be at least forty years old, well old enough for him to be on his own by now. There is something really wrong with this man.*"

"*The police are on their way, and I'm coming up from behind the house. Christ, Weston, this is a beautiful home. I might have the faeries make mine just like this one.*" It was a distraction, something that he only just realized that Jameson was really good at when things were tense. "*I see the moving van. I'm going to have them leave, at least for now, and see what I can do about getting them to pick up his shit."*

"What the hell is he doing?" Weston didn't know what Jameson was doing either, but not only did he get the moving people to gather up the luggage on the front step, but they left without saying a word to him or Hank. The man was really pissed off now. "I suppose you think this is going to get you some kind of out about me moving in. Well, it's just as well that I don't have any furniture. Now I'll have to take yours. See what you've done? Now you have no house, nor do you have anything to put in it."

"Mr. Hathaway, did you know that there is a warrant out for your arrest? The police are on their way as well." Hank asked Jameson why he was being arrested. "Your part in the missing money from the office of Mayor of Dresden. Some of the dealings that I've been able to unearth have your name on them."

"No, that would be my father. Weston here is going to be taking care of things for me. He'll pay whatever fines there are, too. Is he going to be living with you now that you've sent away his moving van?" Jameson didn't answer but looked at the police when they pulled into his drive. "Good. With them here, I can get this all settled up. I need to get out of the heat here, so their timing couldn't be better." He stood up when the first officer came to the porch. "Weston is going to be vacating this house for me. I don't know why you're here, but if you could see your way into getting my things back, I'll not bother you again. Any other things that come up, you can have Weston here take care of them."

"Hank, I'm here to arrest you for trespassing. The Feds are on their way to have a talk with you as well." He again referred them to him to untangle any messes that had come up. "Mr. Sheppard is the acting mayor, not your landlord. You'll come along nicely here, or we'll have to put you in cuffs and take you the hard way."

"You just aren't getting it. He's responsible for my welfare from now on. Especially since he's made sure that my parents are unable to collect from the money they had in the banks." Jameson explained that the money was stolen. "That's just what I've been saying. The money was stolen from them, and now I'm coming here to live in this house since it was Weston who made sure that they were caught. You see? This is nothing that the police need to be involved in. I need to be taken care of, and it's his responsibility to do so."

"No." Weston was getting sick of this and told the man that. "You're not moving into my house. I'm not going to be taking care of you, nor are you going to have a line of credit around town so that you can live in a lifestyle that got your parents into this in the first place." As Hank was being taken away, still telling Weston that he was going to regret this, Rogen and her family showed up.

For a few minutes there, it looked like she was going to knock the shit out of Hank, but in the end, all she managed to do was laugh in Hank's face when he started telling her the same story that he'd been telling him. That he was responsible for him from now on.

~*~

The house was lovelier than she thought it would be. However, after meeting the little people, she understood why the house was changing. It was to suit her. And even though she wasn't sure they should be accommodating her in this, she did enjoy seeing all her dreams in a house come to fruition. It was, simply said, the most beautiful house she'd ever had the pleasure of being inside of.

They toured the upper levels first. The very fact that it had five bedrooms on the second floor made her realize how much she wanted to settle down and have children. It hadn't occurred to her before today how much she wanted a child of her own. And with Weston.

"There is a butler's house on the land. One of the faeries had heard about having one and decided to put one on the land. I have to admit, it's beautiful too, and the gardens around it make me want to eat at home every night just to see what sort of herbs they use on my food." Weston showed her the pantry. "My brother has one too. It came with his home. It's nothing that I would have put in if asked. Are you seeing a lot of homes with them put in nowadays?"

"Quite a few. But they're using it more as

overflow from the kitchen cabinets than things stored for larger parties. The last house that Sandy and I built had two of them put in. One in the kitchen then one in the laundry room for dry goods. I don't know what she was actually going to use it for, but that was what she wanted." He then asked about laundry rooms. "We've put in three in the last few houses. One for the upper floor and then the main floor for the kitchen. Also, one in the garage so that soiled things can be taken care of out there so as not to bring nasty stuff into the house. I have one in the garage where I live, too."

"I can see the need for that. Also, being a shifter, it would be nice to have one out there for things to put on if you were coming home from a good long run." She said that she has a shower for that as well. "Good. Yes, I like that. Do you get to do a lot of long runs as your cat at home?"

"Not nearly as much as I would like. I don't have the land like you guys do here. In fact, last night, I went on a run with my brothers just to chill out. Toby and his family are going to be hard-pressed to leave here when the time comes.

He told me that having all this area is great for his kids, too. I know that his wife, Elizabeth, is enjoying having all the extras around. She loves that she can walk to any place that she needs to go and not have to worry about getting the kids out, too. She's a great mom. I don't know how she does it, what with working full time and taking care of the house and kids."

"I don't have a good role model for that." He told her how his mother pitted him and his brothers against one another all the time and had set out to kill off their mates so that they'd not make her a grandmother. "Our grandda was just as bad at beating us when we didn't do what she wanted us to do. There are some people in town who think that we've done her memory wrong by not being better boys. I don't let them bother me all that much."

By the time they were in the master suite, four rooms just for the master and his mistress of the house, she was about as sappy in love with Weston as she could have been. At one point, she held his hand as they toured the backyard, and she thought that the two of them could make a good family by just being able to hang out with each other. She knew that she wanted to spend the rest of his life with him. Right here in this house.

"I love this place. Its being finished has a lot to do with that. Knowing that I'm not going to have to go home and do something about a wall or a door is nice, too." Weston told her how the faeries were very good at keeping things repaired. "I have to admit having a year-round garden, even though I have no desire to work in one is nice as well. You told me that they made sure you have fresh vegetables and fruits, too, right?"

"We do. I have a cook now. Mae. She'd part faerie and brownie. Brownies tend to be slightly larger than faeries, and it makes it nice that she can organize the magic around the house, too." Weston told her about the walk-in closets and how, when he first got to the house, they were as big as a bedroom. "You have to be careful when you explain to them what it is you want with magic. They tend to think that bigger is better. I do wonder if it's because they're so small, but who knows. You should have seen the barn that Archie wanted put up on the leap land. It was twice the size of the house here. They thought that all the leap was going to live in it and wanted to make it as comfortable as they could for so many. He's since then had them pare it down, but it was funny for a while there."

"Archie did a great job with Belinda getting her money back. We all have taken care of her since our brother was killed. I don't know that she needs us to do that. She's showing us that she likes to take care of herself pretty well." He pointed out that she took good care of him as well. "I heard about the playground equipment men. She had a lot of fun helping you out, she told me."

"I was never really afraid about them. Just getting hurt, but—I forgot to tell you now that we're mates, you're an immortal as well. We can extend that to your family, too, if you'd like. Sunny, she's the daughter of the mother of earth and has somewhat adopted us into her family. Anyway, we can make sure that everyone in your family is safe as well." She didn't know

how she felt about being around for a long time
and told him that. "I'm sure if you didn't want it,
Sunny or her mom could work something out."

"No. I don't want to...I need my family
around me as much as I think you do. They're
my life and my heart." Weston said that he
could understand that, being that he needed his
brothers around him as well. "But you said you'd
move away with me if that was what I wanted?
Do you still believe that?"

"I'll go where you go. I want you to be
as happy as I can make you." She told him that
he was to have some say over where they lived
as well. "I hope you wanted that, but as I said
before, I want you to be happy, and if that means
moving away, then I'm all for it just to be with
you."

They didn't talk all that much more about
leaving after that. She wanted him to be happy
as well, and if that meant she left her family for
him, then so be it. It startled her that after such
a short time with him, she was as willing to give
things up as he'd been. It scared her just a little
to know that the two of them were so suited, too.

"Rogen? Is that your brother-in-law with those kids?" She had to pull herself from her thoughts when he touched his hand to her shoulder. "I don't know what's going on, but it looks to me like he's trying to get them to do something that they're not comfortable with. Do you suppose he's trying to get them into trouble?"

"More than likely." She started toward Danny and the half a dozen kids who were trying their best to back away from him. "What's going on here?"

"Nothing." She told Danny that it didn't look like nothing to her and that the kids looked a little scared. "Oh, them. I was trying to get up a pick-up game, that's all. They're going to be hanging out with me while I'm around town. I got nothing better to do."

"There is plenty that you can do, but you refuse to do it. I spoke with Sandy, and she's going to have you go back home until we're finished here. You're causing us too much trouble not having a sitter all the time." She kept an eye on Weston as the kids disbursed quickly. "What were you going to do with a bunch of kids half your age? Stay away from people, Danny, or so help me, they'll be sending you home in a box. If there is enough of you left to send home."

"You're forever taking me out of my comfort zone." He looked at Weston. "I surely hope that the two of you aren't hooking up. She's a real cunt when it comes to having fun. Or anyone around her having fun too."

"Is that so? I like her kind of fun if it means knocking you around a bit." Weston seemed to grow, and she could see his cat as he ran along his skin. "You talk about my mate like that again, and she won't have a chance to send you home in a box, I'll take care that you're never found around here again. You can count on that."

"I'm only going to ask you once more what you were doing with those kids? Then I'm going to rape your mind to find it." She didn't think that he was going to answer, but when he did, putting just a little compulsion in her voice, she was about as shocked as she'd ever been. "You were going to have them cause an accident at the leap house to kill my sister? Why?"

When Archie suddenly showed up, Danny was put into cuffs and hauled away. She was still reeling about what he'd said about having Sandy killed off when Weston pulled her into his arms. He really wanted her dead? Wanted to kill someone because they weren't allowing him to have all the spending money he wanted? What sort of person did that kind of thing?

Chapter 4

"He thought that once Sandy was dead, then he'd get you to buy out her half of the business, and then he'd be set up for a while. He's also taken out several insurance policies on her that would double if she were to die in an accident." Weston kept an eye on Rogen while she was being told what Danny had planned for her sister. "He didn't see why anyone would care as she wasn't his mate in the first place, and no one would question him. I guess he'd been trying to get someone to do this since before you guys came up here. He thought that it would have been better here because he would be able to manipulate someone else into doing it. Too many people down where you live liked her for him to get away with it."

"I hate to ask this, but did he have anything to do with my brother's death?" Weston knew just when the thought occurred to Rogen, too.

Sandy had been crying, but she seemed to be getting her shit together, as her brothers called it, the longer she sat there listening to what Archie had been able to figure out. Archie nodded. "Christ. What was his reasoning behind that?"

"Money. Insurance. Not to mention, Benson didn't care for the way that Danny was treating his sister and was going to go to the police before he was killed. Belinda was supposed to have been killed as well, we assumed, since he had an insurance policy on her and the kids, too. So far, he's not been able to collect on anything but Benson's. He'd not paid enough into the ones on the children." Weston took Rogen into his arms when she stood up. There was no point in her going to find Danny. Since he was human, he would have to be dealt with by human laws. Mores the pity. "He blew through the money quickly. He doesn't have anything to show for the five hundred grand he'd gotten about a month after the funeral."

"Half a million dollars, and he hasn't anything—that's where he got the games from. The money from killing my brother and my niece and nephew funded his toys so that he could stay at home and do nothing." Sandy looked defeated as if some small part of her felt like she'd been the cause of it all. "He killed them for no other reason than greed. Just like he was planning to do with me. If not for...had we not come here, then everything would have happened just as he planned. We, I have no doubt that he would have killed off all of us one way or another."

The rest of the evening was spent quietly talking about anything but Danny. There were plenty of tears. Some memories were brought up about little incidents about things they were only just realizing.

"I'll gladly go to prison for killing him." That was the second time one of the Watsons said that, and he believed them just as much. "He killed our brother, and there was no reason for it."

After a while, Archie and Sunny decided to have dinner brought in. There was plenty of food, and people seemed to be eating, but there was none of the cheerfulness that came with family getting together. Once it was established that there wasn't any way for the family to get to Danny on their own, he was in jail surrounded by police. They began talking about the other projects that he had going on, from the school building to the mayor's office, that needed to be worked on as well. Even a little of the conversation was about Hank and his odd conversations about him having to take care of him.

By dessert, the two families were beginning to get pissed off, not at each other but at Danny. They'd gone from the grief stages to the pissed-off one in record time. It was agreed that as soon as they could, they'd go to the police station and file charges against the other man.

"The men from the leap that he'd been trying to convince to kill Sandy are coming forward. He offered them five hundred dollars apiece to cut her lines on her break lines or to make sure that she was using faulty equipment on the job site. The circular saw was to be faulty enough where she'd just suffered enough that he could milk it when she finally died." Weston asked Jameson if he'd told the family that. "Not yet, but it will come out. One of the men recorded the conversation with him without his knowledge. He turned it over to Archie this afternoon, and I'm only just now hearing about it."

"Christ, this is a nightmare. I suppose asking her for a divorce wouldn't have even occurred to him." He explained about the business. "So he thought that he'd be able to get half the earnings from that even though his wife was deceased? He's a sick fuck if you were to ask me. We've been really broke before, but I don't think any of us have thought about killing one another off for money. Why didn't he get a job?"

"I believe you know the answer to that without asking." He did. But it was just too far-fetched for him to think that anyone could be that lazy about things. "What else do you know? I mean, is there more that the family is going to have to deal with?"

"Nothing that has come to me. But I would keep an eye on the women. Not because I think that he might have gotten someone to take her out but simply because they'll hurt him, if not kill him soon." There was that, and while he wouldn't blame them, he didn't want them to go to prison for a man like Danny. "Also, Toby approached me the other day, and he's thinking about moving here. He said it's wonderful for his family, and I think that if he stays, the others will as well. Especially after all this."

It was a lot to think about right now. He wanted to whisk Rogen away and tell her that he had her, but knew that it was important for her to be with her family right now. There were other things going on, too. Not even related to Danny and his mess that he needed to be on top of. Like Hank.

He was telling anyone who would listen that he'd okayed for him to live with him. Anyone who knew him knew it for a lie, but the people who were still supporting his mother and grandfather were starting up again. Talking like it would be something that he'd do, invite someone to stay then tell them no. Hank also knew where his parents were and wasn't talking. They could hold him in the cell for a bit longer because of that, but he didn't know what he'd do when the man got out. He, as his aunt said, had his cheese slip off his cracker.

Pulling out his laptop to work while the Watson family planned — what he didn't know, but he was going to make sure that he had bail money when it was necessary — he decided that he could get a little work done before he had to go home. Just as he was pulling up a file, Rogen came to sit with him.

"I want to move here. With you." He told her that would be fine with him and did she want the house he'd built. "Just like that, you'll be all right with me moving in? What about my murdering brother? Do you take that into account, too?"

"First, he's not your brother. He was never related to you or any of you. And only to Sandy marginally. Second, I've been in love with you since I first laid eyes on you and could care less if you have fifty murderers in your family. It's you I love, and the others can suck off if they wish." He laughed at the expression on her face. "Did you expect me to just turn you down because of one idiot? Danny won't be around much longer, and that's about all I can stand of him. Now, do you want the house or not? I'm willing to rebuild or buy anything that you want."

"I want the house. What if I told you that the others have decided to move here as well? By the way, I'm worried about Belinda. She said it's like having her family murdered all over again with this coming out." Weston said he could understand that, and he was fine with all of them living around here. "Will your family give them a good deal on the houses that they're renting out for us? I'm to understand that Sunny owns them all."

"According to Sunny, we own them as a family. And yes, if she doesn't give them to them, I'll help them buy them. I have enough money for that." Rogen nodded. "What else did you want to tell me or ask me? You look like you have a lot to say."

"I don't, not really. I'm worried. What if he gets out? Danny won't last long if he does. It won't be a matter of if he gets killed but who gets to him first to do the deed. He's done enough to us as it is, and for some reason, him sitting in a jail cell and being taken care of pisses me off to no end." He told her what he'd heard from his brother. "So they're not giving in to his demands. I would hope that they don't do that anyway."

"He's not getting any kind of treatment. Like when his meal is ready, they'll wait until it's cold before they serve it to him. No extra blankets either. His cot has a missing leg, and they have ignored his requests for a new one. Little things that are making his like hell being in jail. Oh, and the phone is broken. He can't call anyone, meaning he can't call the family for help with getting himself an attorney, either. And Archie is making sure that he's getting nothing in return for his 'help' on having you jailed. He said this is all your fault."

"How the hell is this all my fault?" He explained what he'd heard from the office. "So because my sister couldn't give him a child, even though he'd been told about that before, it's my fault that he had to kill my brother and his kids? That's the stupidest thing I've ever heard. What else is he saying?"

"It's funny, really. He thinks that your brothers are only farmers because they're too stupid to do anything else. Also, and this one I find really funny, you go to him for advice on how to do your job. He said he should be getting a consulting fee or something. He's actually telling people that one the most. And, he needs for you to get him some money so that he can grease some palms in the jail so he can get things going. The thing he's requested most is a cell phone. I don't even want to think about what he'd do if he had one of them."

"He'd hire a hit on us all." He didn't even blink at her when she suggested that was what he'd do. Because that was exactly what he was doing even in the jail system. "He wants us dead."

"Just you. For now." She nodded and asked for him to tell her. "He believes that you're the one that controls the family and that they do what you tell them. That's the reason that Sandy wouldn't do what he wanted, and the others agreed. He said that you should have bought her out so that she could stay at home with him and cater to his every need. Children were mentioned, but he said that he's manly enough to be able to make it work with Sandy having them a few kids. He's talking about welfare and the benefits that are there for him to get if he has a lot of children. The man is off his noodle if you ask me."

"Or he's really smart. Could he be playing that he's really stupid to get out of jail? I've heard it happen before." Weston said that he'd not thought of that. "I think we might want to think about anything and everything concerning him. If we don't, then he's going to make some waves that even killing him won't take away."

"I'll have my brothers look into things. You might have a brilliant idea." She sat there long enough for him to talk to his brother, Jameson. He was a young attorney, just passing his bar in the last few months, but he was smart in that he never let anything get by him. He had an idea that Rogen might be onto something and left to go and look into things. "He said he likes the way that you think. Outside the box, so to speak."

"I've been around a lot of people that will try their best to take advantage of you. It's why I've been very careful of what I allow humans to do and not do. My friendliness only goes so far before I cut them off." He never would have thought of her as jaded and said as much to her. "I don't know that I'd call me jaded, but more like I'm not as trusting as most are. Sandy is. Or she was very trusting. I don't think any of us will be that much after all this."

They talked about the plans he had for the office he was in. She had some ideas too about how to make improvements around town that wouldn't cost so much. Getting people involved in their own town was something that she had her heart set on in her other town. She didn't think it was so different here, either.

"Have a yard décor contest for the holidays. That's one way to get people involved. There doesn't have to be a big money value, just their picture in the paper with their home. A lot of people take pride in their homes that no one around them understands. Planting a few flowers even will go a long way in making the streets look good for people coming around when you're flirting for new businesses." He wrote down all the things that she was saying.

"Also, if you have decorations stored away for street lights and stuff, people will help you out with those too. Have a parade or something. That'll bring in other family members just to see their cousin or something on a big float. It doesn't cost all that much, and it's fun for the families."

She had a lot of good ideas on how to make a town spruced up. He was all for that. It had occurred to him that gardens, too, would be a good way to get people involved. Having a farmers market too would certainly bring in some fun, too. As he was making notes, he noticed that the Watsons had grown quiet. Asking him what was going on, she told him that they were going to find them places to work and were going over the newspaper that was in his living room. Weston thought that it was as good as any place to start.

~*~

It was the first time in longer than she could remember that Rogen was out running with someone other than just her family. Having the Sheppards out with them, all of them running through the wooded area, was like being free of the burden—at times, it felt like that—but just being free of being part human.

After running for a good solid hour, she was ready to stretch out and enjoy the sun beating down on her skin. The first thing she did when she found herself a nice spot was stretch out her cat and her claws. Even getting dirt in them didn't make her any less satisfied with what she'd been able to do.

"Where did you go?" She smiled when she heard from her sister, Sandy. *"I have to be honest with you, Rog. This is the first time I've felt like a real person in a long time. Even being a cat, I feel like I could take on the world. I'm glad that Weston suggested it."*

"I am too, but I think that he only meant for the two of us to go, but I believe he's having the time of his life as well. We all needed this." Sandy agreed with her. *"I was just thinking about how seldom we get to do this at home. Toby said it had been years since he'd been running. I know what he means. I shift to give my cat some freedom, but nothing like this. No wonder they don't want to leave this area. I don't either."*

There were nearly two hundred acres around the houses that they could roam in. The Sheppards all had homes going up around the area, too, but it was mostly trees and deep scrub they were playing in. The pond was a long, rambling one that seemed to be in the middle of all the land that her cat had played in for nearly twenty minutes before running after Archie when he came and splashed her in the face. It was a treat that she'd not expected and loved all the more because of it.

"I have a question for you to ask Weston." She told Sandy that she could ask him if she wanted something. *"I could, but he'd just tell me to ask you or something, and I want this in the worst sort of way. I want to have the butler's home behind your house. I don't want a big house, I don't want to live far from you, and I think that it's the perfect place for me to be. Deep enough in the woods so that no one will bother me either."*

"I don't care if you take it, but it really is off the beaten path. Are you sure you'd rather not have a little house nearer to town?" She told her why she didn't want to live in the town. *"I doubt very much*

people will care that you were married to Danny, honey. They're going to be more than likely ready to take you under their wing rather than blame you for something that you had nothing to do with."

"I just want to be alone for a while. I'm not saying that I want to live out my life in solitude, but for now, I want to...I guess you could call it reflect on what I've done to put me in this mood. He really did take us all for a ride, didn't he?" He had to. And the worst part was, he'd profited off their sorrow. "I was sort of afraid that Belinda would blame me for all this, but she told me that I was supposed to get that notion out of my head. That he did this all on his own, and that's all there is to it."*

She had said as much to her about Sandy as well. And that he would have done it to another family had it not been theirs but with them, he was caught before it got too far. He would have killed more of them if not for the fact that Weston had figured out what he'd been up to. She would have been—

"I'm going to bond with Weston as soon as possible. Life is too short for me to be waiting for the right time. We both love each other, so what the hell* *am I waiting on."* She, like Weston, had fallen in love quickly. Probably because they were both cats, she didn't know, but she wanted to be with him for the rest of her life and damn this waiting game to see if it was going to last. *"I've been a fool in waiting around for the other shoe to drop. He's been so sweet in waiting for me to come around. Not once has he pressured me, either. Just being my mate and waiting on me to shit or get off the pot."*

"You have such a way with words, love." They both laughed as she was lying in the sun drenched field. Curling into a nice ball of fur, she rolled to her back so that the sun was hitting her in all the right places. *"I see you now. Can I join you? That looks so inviting."*

She wanted to nap alone but knew too that once Sandy was with her, she'd not jabber on and on until she wanted to smack her. Before she could tell her that she wanted quiet time, Sandy was snoring slightly and rolled into a nice ball, too.

When she woke, she was alone in the field. She didn't know when Sandy had left but was glad that she'd not bothered her when leaving.

Stretching out again, her fur standing on end, she shifted to her other self and was happy to know that one of the perks that you got in finding your mate was true. She was fully clothed in the things that she'd had on before. Standing up, she made her way to the little house in the clearing that she'd not noticed before. It had to be the butler's house that Sandy was talking about, and she was glad that it was in as good a shape as she hoped it would be.

"Mistress, would you like for me to make the house open for you?" She told Syrup, the little red faerie that had helped her before, that she'd loved that, then told him about what her sister wanted. "Oh, she'll love it here. There are a number of faeries around, that she won't be alone entirely. They'll keep her safe, too."

"Have you heard about her husband and what he was planning to do?" Syrup told her that all the faeries knew and felt so sorry for the young mistress. "She thinks that people will not like her being around because of what he's done to our family."

"There was a troll once that decided to kill

his wife and children because he couldn't be the monster that he wanted when the queen was looking for guards of the realm. He didn't, of course, but it wasn't because of a lack of trying. Trolls make the best guards for the queen, and she pays them very well. I still, to this day, have no idea how he was going to make it work. He was a lazy person and didn't work when his wife did. But this troll, Quarter, was his name, and he didn't want to be married to such a person as he was married to, either. I don't know what it was about his mistress that he didn't like, she was much like him, a troll, but she came from a poor family and was forever making him watch his money. He thought that all money was there to spend and that she was wrong in keeping him from his play." She told Syrup that he sounded like Danny, Sandy's husband. "Yes, I thought that you'd see that. Quarter tried all kinds of ways to rid himself of his family—they don't mate and find their only one like shifters do. They fall in love, or so everyone thinks, and that they are together forever. But he was a monster, even going so far as to try and sell his children to humans for them to do things to. Can you imagine what a human would do with such a thing as a troll child? It gives me the willies to think on it."

"Did the queen find out?" She was just entering the house when Weston joined her. Smiling at him, she told him what Syrup was telling her about. "I hope that someone took him to task or, at the very least, had him go to jail."

"He is no longer with us." She knew that to kill a troll, or so she had read, was difficult. They were thick-skinned and mean. Wondering how this particular being was killed, she paused in the doorway to the little house to ask him what had happened. "His lady mistress came upon him trying to murder her son, and she tore his head off. You should see the rooms above, my lady. They had a splendid view of the forest beyond here."

"I'm sorry, you said she ripped his head off?" Syrup nodded and said that she had indeed. Her anger was so powerful. "What happened to her? Did the queen punish her?"

"No, she'd never do that. She gave her

a little house for her and her sons, and they're making grass rugs to use in the faerie homes. I have two of them in my own home. She makes them bigger for shifters, too. They're quite beautiful; however, even if they were ugly, I don't believe anyone would tell her. She had ripped the head off a full-grown troll, you know." Rogen looked at Weston. She was happy to see that he was as shocked as she was about what the little man had said. "Shall I tell her that you'd like one of them too?"

She couldn't help it. She burst out laughing. When Weston joined her, she held onto him as their mirth got the better of them. It was said so nonchalantly that she couldn't believe the story. While she knew it was true, the faeries didn't lie, but it was the way that he sprinkled in bits about the house that got her going. Every time she looked at him, too, she would have a bit of laughter spill from her lips.

While they toured the house, she told him what Sandy had wanted. Weston, who she knew he would, was all for it, and he even suggested that the house be able to change for her needs, too. It was something that she'd forgotten about in her own home, and was glad that he suggested it. Having Sandy so close would do a lot for her well-being, too. Her sister was her world.

As they walked home, they didn't say all that much. He would point out things that he saw, and she would question him about things that she did. Rogen hadn't realized how close the houses were until they went on their run. All the brothers were having their homes built by the faeries, and they were going up quickly. She hoped they didn't do that too much, or she'd be out of a job soon.

For the rest of the afternoon and into the evening, the two of them lazed around the house. She read some of a book that she'd been wanting to read, and Weston did a crossword puzzle. As dinner rolled around they were deciding on what to have when their cook asked them if they wished to grill out. It sounded so good to her that she had ideas of all the food that could be put on the grill and cooked the quickest. She was suddenly that hungry.

Ending up with steaks on the grill and

grilled veggies, she was finished with her steak before she'd finished the rest of her meal. When asked if she wanted a second one, both she and Weston agreed. All the sunshine and running as their cats had given them quite an appetite, it seemed. She even had a second baked potato, she'd been so starved.

After dinner, almost too full to move, the two of them sat out on the deck on the back of their home. The night was dark, with hardly any stars out, but it was the perfect night to sit outside and not be bothered by anyone. She didn't even think of her family either. It was just the two of them.

"I have a meeting in the morning with the Feds. They've found some money that I can have to work on some of the projects that were left undone. They're suggesting the school, but I've been there, and it's the jail that needs the most immediate work on it. Like a fresh building and cells." She asked him if they'd hire locally to do the work. "Of course. I have to put in bids, but I was hoping that you and your sister would be there to work on it as well. For it to be done right."

"I don't know how that works. Usually, we just build or remodel homes. But I'm thinking that if someone puts in a bid, they'll have their own contractor to oversee the project." He said he didn't know how it worked either. "I can help you with the blueprints, however. I have a friend of mine who designs buildings for city work. I could give him a call. I think that if you have a plan in mind, you can figure out who is going to give you the best price that way."

The two of them ended up looking up how to put out a bidding contract for the jail and learned a great deal about it. By the time they were ready for bed, she'd contacted her friend, and they were well on their way to having a new jail built for the town.

Chapter 5

Rogen had had enough waiting for him to make the first move. He had told her that he'd wait on her to make it, but she thought that he'd been joking. This was no longer funny. Nor did she find it fulfilling. She wanted him, and he was going to fuck her or else. Finding him in his office, she didn't hesitate to make her needs known to him.

"I want to have sex with you. I don't care where or anything like that, but I'd like to have it soon. I'm sick of waiting." Weston told her, no, he'd not have sex with her. "What do you mean, no? We're mates. We're supposed to have lots of sex. At least, that's what I've been told. Is there something wrong with me?"

"No, nothing wrong. I did tell you that I wouldn't rush you since you were living in this house. But I want to make love with you. Not sex, not fucking but making love." She asked him what the difference was. "Sex is a mutual coming together to get your rocks off. I'm not saying that making love isn't the same thing, but it will be to me. I don't want to fuck you either. That sounds like we're strangers just getting together for a mutual gain. While that is too something that I want, I don't want you that way. I want to taste you, your skin, and your breath. I want to feel your skin quiver under my fingers, your body to respond to mine. I want you to need me to complete you. To have you come when I do. That's what I want and more."

Moving toward him, she didn't know if she wanted to smack him or take him. Looking at the desk he'd been sitting at, she wondered if it would hold them up for the kind of fucking that she wanted. And she did want him. In the worst sort of way, she could get him.

"Yes...I, please. Please, Weston." She gripped his shoulders, and, lifting one leg up then the other, she wrapped them around his hips, anchoring her ankles at his back, and began riding him harder, tighter with his help. "This is what I want. To feel you making love to me like

I'm everything in the world to you."

"You are everything in the world to me. You have been since the day I met you. I've wanted to claim you, to make you mine in any way that I could. I love you, Rogen Sheppard. And I will for the rest of my life, too." She pulled her blouse off and tossed it to the floor. "More. I want to see all of you, please."

She just stared at him. Her mind was confused while her body was full of lust. It was at that moment when she knew that he'd never leave her. Why? She didn't know where those thoughts came from, but she knew deep in her heart that Weston would care for her forever and a day.

"I want to come all over you, love. I want to take this first time slowly for you. Taste you, as I said. Make love to you, heart and soul." Nodding, she moved closer to him. Her body, though she was clothed, was in desperate need of his touch, his breath...just as he'd said, she wanted him to make love to her.

Reaching down, she undid his pants, pulling the zipper over his hardening cock was hard. There was a slight wetness to his briefs, and he made her hungry for more of him. Just his touch wasn't enough. Rogen wanted all of him now.

As she watched him, he wrapped his hand around his shaft and pumped his hand up and down. A drop of cum seeped from the tip. It was what she needed to make the movement slick and fast while she joined him at his cock. She could barely get her hands fully around him. His shaft was so thick.

Licking her lips, a need to take him into her mouth made her hungry and aggressive. She started forward, her head bent to take him into her mouth, reaching for him, and he stopped her. Her heart, beating hard in that moment, seemed to shatter. But when she looked up at him, his smile was pure sin. Her pussy seemed to swell then, and she wanted Weston to take her hard.

Moving toward him, slowly and with purpose, she put her hands on his shoulders and looked up at him. Weston was all she ever wanted in a man, and she nearly forgot that. He was the best thing that had ever happened to her.

~*~

Weston knew that they weren't going to last long if they were both naked. Instead of pulling her clothing free, all he did was push her breast up until it spilled out of the bra, and he was happy when it bounced slightly.

Her nipple was pink and tight. As much as he wanted to savor the sight, need pushed him forward, and he took her into his mouth and suckled the firm flesh. He suckled hard and firmly, pulling the tight nub in as deeply as he could into his mouth until she wrapped her hands into his hair and pulled him back. When he scraped his teeth gently over the swollen peak, he drew a tiny drop of blood. As he licked the tiny wound, tasting her, Rogen tossed back her head and came apart, screaming her sudden release.

He held her to him as she began to settle, his body screaming for its own release, but not now, he thought, not without the bed beneath them. He wasn't going to take his mate for the first time on the floor. Because after his first taste of her skin, the first lick across her warmth, he knew he'd found his true mate.

His cock was hard and aching to have her. To fill her up as much as he could. Stripping down to nothing and tearing at her own clothing as he stood there, he stood before her as a man in love and one with a need only she could help him with. When she reached for him, he took a small step back.

"No. Not yet. I would like nothing better than to have you wrap your mouth around me, but I want to taste you more. Next time, I promise you'll be able to do what you want, but next time. Oh sweetheart, you're wet, so wet I can see the dampness on your curls." He let go of his cock and touched her pussy with his nimble fingers. As much as he wanted to roll his eyes in the back of his head, he didn't because he didn't want to miss a single thing in their making love for the first time.

His finger moved slowly along her nether lips, up and down like he had his cock when they'd been dressed. The friction was nearly too much, but she held onto him. Her body responded, and he could smell her pussy weep more. He hadn't touched her yet, not touched her where she needed, he knew, but it was getting harder and harder for him to wait for her and the right time. When his finger slowly entered her heat, she opened her legs wider and raised her hips up to meet him. He could have come in that moment.

"Please, Weston. I want you. I...there's a need, something...I don't...you have to fill it for me, please, fill me before I die." Her hips moved up and down with his finger, and when he inserted another into her, she nearly came up off the bed. Whimpering now, she moved faster with his fingers. It was what she wanted in that moment and more. She wanted him to touch her like she was something or someone special. To take her breath away when he kissed her.

"I need to stretch you love. You're too tight to take me inside of you yet. I don't want to hurt you in any way. That's what you want, isn't it? For me to fill you with my cock?" He was moving faster now; her body was on fire where he could feel it. To form words would have been too much for him to imagine. Yes, he screamed in her mind. The connection between them was stronger now.

"Yes, oh yes, please." He felt rather than saw her move, her body straining to get to something more from him. Moving them to the bed, making sure that she was in the middle where he could have his fun, Weston kissed his way to her hips and beyond. Christ, he wanted her so badly.

When he kissed her thigh, she started to clamp her legs closed, but he held them open with his hands and fingers. She was panting now. He could hear her, their need for each other making him ache for release.

With his fingers, he opened her nether lips and ran his tongue inside her, lapping at her, tasting her she knew. When his mouth closed over her clit and suckled into his mouth, she screamed out her climax filling his mouth with her juices, but he didn't stop. While his fingers fucked her, his mouth teased and nipped at her until she came again and again.

"Please, Weston, please. I want you. I want to suck your cock. Now. I want you to come in my mouth." As she reached for him, pulling away from his very talented tongue, she pushed him back against the footboard. She leaned forward and stroked the length of him with just the tips of her fingers. His hiss made her bolder.

"Take me, love. Take me in your mouth. I want to fuck your hot mouth and shoot cum deep into your throat." It took her a few moments to get into a position to do what he wanted.

She swiped her tongue across the tip of the large, deep purple head, taking the cream into her mouth. He hissed again. Bolder than she had ever been in her life, she wrapped her lips around him and licked again. She loved the way he responded. He pumped into her.

While she didn't know what she was doing but, taking her cues from him and his body, she licked and nipped every inch of him, up one side of him, then down the other of his long, stiff shaft. When she felt his hand touch the back of her head, she felt him guide her, show her what he needed. Soon he was pumping into her hard, his cock bumping the back of her throat again and again.

"I'm going to come to Rogen. Fuck, I'm coming!" Seconds later, she felt the first hot explosion hitting the back of her throat. He pumped harder into her, pulsing into her over and over. She swallowed him, his cum. Loving the salty taste that she knew was unique to him. He lifted her up and turned her over onto her hands and knees. She was ready, she thought, so ready for his cock to be deep inside of her. Moaning, she moved back against him.

He licked his tongue across the skin at her shoulder that was caught between his teeth and moaned as he nipped at her skin. He released the holding bite, and moved his mouth along her bare shoulder, and nuzzled his mouth against the point of her neck that met the shoulder. He kissed the warm, silky skin and nipped at the pulse beating there. Need, his need to mate, dominating her thought process completely. Even if she could have had a thought.

He felt her move beneath him, her fingers gripping his hand. Moving his mouth lower, he followed the vein along her throat, and then he stopped at the base of her neck. Her own moan vibrated along her throat against his mouth. He ran his hands down her arms, caressing them as he went. His tongue licked the area there, taking more of her taste into his mouth. His body leaned closer to her, and his legs tightened around her as he gently covered her with his length. He ran his tongue up the length of her neck, moving along her hot blood as he went.

When his mouth met her jaw, he moved up and gently swept his mouth against hers, brushing his lips across the fullness of hers, the heat. Once, then again, breathing her in as he went back and forth until he felt her respond to him. He nipped at her bottom lip and suckled it into his mouth, pulling more of her flavor into his mouth. He pulled back an inch and looked into her eyes, waiting for her to look back at him.

When their eyes met, Weston slowly moved the last inch to her mouth and rocked against her core with his cock. Moving his right hand down her ribs, he slipped it beneath her, spreading his hand wide, pressing her to him. His left hand moved to her head and, angling her head, held her to him as he kissed her. His mouth covered hers as he rolled over and brought her body over his, cradling her between his legs.

He moved his hands down her ribs and cupped her ass, pulling her tight against his hard cock. Moaning deep, he reached further, never breaking contact with the sweetness of her mouth, and grasped her thighs. Tugging her up and widening her legs, he settled them along his own hips this time. When she moved against him on her own and began riding him, he sat up, bringing her with him. They were chest to chest now.

Grasping her hips, he moved her faster and harder against him. He slipped his hand to the hem of her shirt and pulled it up over her head, and tossed it aside. He felt her fingers move along the buttons of his shirt as he cupped her breast, still covered in the scrap of material of her bra. Pressing them together, he ran his thumb over the stiff peaks of her nipples as she ran her fingers through the hair on his chest.

"Rogen, baby. I want to suckle; I need to suckle your breast in my mouth." His voice had deepened; he felt that as much as he heard it. I need to be inside of you as well. Please let me take you."

He didn't wait for an answer but lifted her hips up from behind as he took her. Almost as soon as he entered her pussy, he came apart.

The pain took its time being known to him. Each time he took a breath, he could feel it moving over him. He knew what it was. It was his claiming his mate. It was then that he realized that this could be happening to her as well, and he reached for Rogen.

She wasn't close to him, not close enough for him to touch anyway. When she cried out, her whimpering voice telling him that she was hurting too, Weston wanted to go to her and help her, but it wasn't to be. He was writhing in his own pain right now and could barely contain his own screams.

His cat cried out and then curled tightly around his body. It was the first time in his life that he'd ever thought of his cat as someone other than a part of him. When he moved, stretching out his claws to grab at something other than the air, Weston knew a new kind of pain when, again, he met with nothing more than air.

Waking up, he was in his bed, but he was terrified to move, fearful of whatever kind of fresh pain might be brought to him. Rogen lay beside him, but she wasn't moving either. He was sure of what happened but not of what had caused it.

"The faeries said that we were to lie here for another hour. I'm all for that, but they seemed to be overly worried that we're going to be getting up and moving around." He asked Rogen who she had spoken to. "Syrup. What an adorable name. He said that our bodies are going to take time to adjust to what has happened to us. What did happen to us?"

"To be honest, I'm not sure. I feel like I've been wrung out and then left in the sun to dry. How are you feeling?" She told him that was pretty much the way that she felt as well. But more on the hung out to dry in a blizzard. "You're cold?" Weston thought about it for a moment. "You know what? I am, as well. I don't think I've ever been cold since the first time that I shifted."

"Who put us in bed? I mean, we were naked when we fell to the floor." He didn't remember falling to the floor but didn't say anything. Wiggling his toes, he felt like he was pulling muscles from his head just to do that little bit of work. "You were told not to move, smart ass. Just lie still."

"I have to pee." She laughed at him then, telling him that she'd had to go for the last ten minutes. "Well, if I don't get up soon, we're going to have to get a new bed. I really need to get up."

After swinging his legs off the bed, he had to lay there for an additional ten minutes. It wasn't as if he hurt; he didn't hurt any longer, but he was exhausted. He wanted to blame it on the most incredible sex he'd ever had, but he also knew that couldn't be all that. He was just about as tired as he'd ever been.

When he was finally able to get up from the bed, he staggered, holding onto things as he made his way there. Once he was in the bathroom, he had to hold onto the sink or fall face-first into the commode. After using the toilet, washing his hands felt like it was too much. The sensation of water running over his fingers was akin to having his body turned inside out again. He barely made it back to the bed before he was ready for a long nap.

Waking up the next time, he was glad to see that Rogen was sleeping, too. He felt better than he had before, not nearly as exhausted, so when he got up to use the bathroom again, he didn't have to hold onto things as he made his way back. Sitting on the side of the bed, he contemplated getting himself dressed or taking another nap. He convinced himself that getting up might cost him something, but he couldn't lie around in bed all day when he had work to do.

The second time he made his way to the bathroom to shower, he did feel better. Rogen was still sleeping, so he took his shower quietly. If anyone were to ask him, he'd tell them that he was straight up fine when, in reality, he was just like a newborn, too tired to think beyond lying down again.

The kitchen was full of activity when he got there. Apparently, Mae, the cook, was helping the faeries make more jam and jelly. He didn't know how well dandelion jelly was going to go over, but he did take a taste and thought that it was delicious. While he was being given his breakfast, Rogen joined him in the vast room.

"There are several things that have come up. Which would you like to hear first?" Pancake and Syrup were running point it seemed on things that they were to take care of. "The mistress of the lands, our queen, wishes a word with the two of you when you are up to it. She seemed to think that it would be a couple of days, but we were going to remind you when you felt better. I had not known you were ill. Is there anything that I can do to help you, sir?"

"I'm fine and am ready when you are to tell me what's been going on." He told him how Hank had been released in order to be watched in the event that he went to his parent's home. "He isn't coming here again, is he?"

"No. We have taken care that he will not come here again. We've made it so that he has forgotten that he wishes to live with you. For now, he is content to live in one of the hotels in town. They know too not to allow him to go without paying. Some of our kind have been running the business for some time now." Weston nodded and asked why they thought that he'd go to his parents. "Mistress Sunny has made him think that it is vital that he finds them for his wellbeing. I'm not sure how that magic works, but she does have us keeping both our eyes on him, so he can't leave without one of us following him."

He did have a moment of humor rolling over him, thinking about how that conversation went about them keeping both their eyes on the man. The faeries were the best to have around, but they could also be the worst. He did so enjoy their ways of thinking too.

The rest of the news they had was things that were going on in the rest of the family. Archie had finally been able to move into the new leap house with his offices. The rules that he had for his own leap were making their way to all the people who were a part of it, too. The teaching of the leap too was going well as they were getting more work done, too.

"What do you know of the money from the Feds? Has anyone talked to them about it?" Syrup said that while the money wasn't in the bank as yet, he knew that it was coming. He even knew how much was coming and told them so. "Good. That's really good. We've already started getting someone to build the jail for us, so now we can talk to the people about the schools. There is a lot of work needed to be done for both places."

By the time he was finished with his breakfast, he had another long list of things that he needed to get started on. The school was going to be built in the summer months so that there wouldn't be any disruption to the class time. Also, they were going to be using some of the storage units that were being built to put the things in it that the new school wouldn't use. Chalkboards and some of the other outdated items would be sold at auction at a later date. In addition to the things from the classroom, there would be things like the outbuildings that had been brought in to use for classes that would be sold as well. Little things and big things that would sell off, and all the money would go to the teachers to use to make their school rooms look good for the students. He liked that idea a great deal.

"The playground equipment has arrived." He asked where the money came from for that. It had been put off until more money was found from the other mayor's theft. "It was donated by the queen. It doesn't say that on the invoice, but she did want to make sure that the children had plenty of things to have fun with in the warmer months. Children make their own kind of magic that we all get something from."

Sitting in his office nearly two hours after he'd gotten up, Weston was ready for a long nap again. It wasn't that he was that tired, but he was beginning to feel like he'd run a marathon. Just getting his computer turned on, Leanord, Rogen's brother, showed up. He would do anything for her family, and even being busy, he'd drop everything to help them out.

"I want to find some farm that I can purchase. I have a buyer for ours at home. We all want to move here." He told him that he knew of three farms that were up for sale, and then he asked him how much land he wanted. "Enough that Toby and I can farm it together. Enough, too, that we can hire some hands to help us out when the time is right. Having our equipment shipped here is going to save us a great deal of money, but we need to have enough land to support us and make the payments on the tractors and other equipment that we have."

Weston had heard that some of the farming tractors that his new family had were expensive, but he'd not thought that they'd be in the millions of dollars for everything that they had. He could also understand why they were having it brought here rather than to sell it off and start again. That alone made him think that the Watson brothers were bigger farmers than he thought they were. He also liked the idea that the two of them were thinking of staying in business so that they could provide for their families.

Weston went with the two of them, both Toby and Leanord, to look over the land. Most of the fields hadn't been plowed in a decade, the expense being too much in this town. The two properties that they were most interested in were going on the auction block in a few days, and them having all the specs ready certainly helped them with information about the land.

"I'm thinking that we could get a better deal by going to the auction rather than through the bank. I know they have a minimum on it, but it's not nearly as much as they're asking for the land." Weston had to let them work out the numbers for the land as he'd never had to deal with it before. "I think that if we wait too, we can get some of the equipment that is being sold off too. Did you know that one of the ranches is selling off their standing cattle, too?"

"I'm sorry to say that I don't know much about what is going on in my little town." Toby told him that wasn't anything to be sorry for. If he didn't know, then he simply didn't know. "You're right, of course, but I wish I could be more of a help to you about this."

"You have been. Not just with this but with our sisters, too. Getting them started on some of the houses around here is going to make this a family effort. My wife is a teacher, and she's hoping to be able to teach here in the fall. You've provided us with housing, which I don't know if you're aware of this or not, but it has made it easier for us to decide that we want to be nearer to Belinda and Rogen. You've done a lot for us, Weston. A great deal more than we've ever had from our previous town mayor." He thanked him. "Now, if you could get us the information on your brother to join his leap, we'll have everything that we need to get things finalized for us living here."

Weston laughed when Toby told him that he was joking. It had already been set up for them to join the leap, and as far as he knew, they were also joining other things around town. The council for the town, a sort of nosey bunch that had their hands into everything, was now going to be run by Belinda, and he couldn't have been happier about it.

They met up with Beau as he was leaving the YMCA from one of his classes. He was learning how to cook. Not to be a big-time chef or anything, but so that he could cook a meal for himself and his family if it came to it. He, in turn, was teaching Jameson and Nash how to cook, too. This week, he was learning how to grill vegetables on the grill and how to know when a steak was done. Things that he didn't know either.

"I've been thinking about what you told me the other day." He'd not known that Beau had been hanging out with the other two men. But then, Beau had always been the most social of all of them. "You were telling me that I could raise a couple of goats to get to my lawn, and I like that idea. Also, what you told me about them keeping some of the vining troublesome weeds out of my area."

"We're going to have goats for that same reason." Toby laughed. "There is also the benefit that my wife wants to see about making goat cheese for us. She's always been the one who could squeeze a dollar until it screamed. But she figures that since we have to have them anyway, why not profit off of them for some cheese. My kids love goat cheese."

Toby had four kids, all of them under the age of ten, and he seemed to be the happiest man

he'd ever met. Also a great dad. There was never
a time when he wasn't out in the yard with one of
them having some fun. Weston wanted to have
children, too, but he was going to be a great dad
like his new brother-in-law. Toby was the best.

Chapter 6

Carrie didn't want to bring attention to herself while the three ghosts that were arguing finished up whatever they were doing. She knew who they were, why they were with her, and who had killed them. But she couldn't tell them anything unless they figured it out for themselves. As it stood right now, she didn't figure that they'd ever get to that point, and she wasn't going to be telling them anything until then. It had been several months now, and they were still fighting amongst themselves like she was sure they'd done when they were alive. The older of the three of them turned to her, but she didn't let her see that she wanted to be elsewhere. Ghosts could be mean at times, and she didn't feel like messing with them today.

"You there. Are you going to just sit there, or are you going to help us sort this out?" She told the elder woman, Helen Pine, that she was waiting on them. "Waiting for what? You need to get us something to eat and drink while we figure out where Howard is. He should be here too."

"I'm not going to do anything until you figure this out on your own. I've said that to you several times now, and until you do, you're going to just stand where you are." They had to be where they were because it was the house they'd been killed in. This house, one that had been well kept, was a place they'd been squatting in for the past several weeks. Then, for some reason, Howard Pine, Helen's son, had had enough of them and had killed not just his mother but his father and grandfather. "I don't think that Howard is coming back here either."

Howard had been killed several counties over by the police when he tried to rob a convenience store. He'd been on his way out of town when he'd made his fatal decision. Sunny joined her in the room just as she was thinking about leaving them to their business.

"I thought that you had hours set up for them to come and see you." She explained how these people had been murdered three months ago and still hadn't figured out that they were dead. "Does it usually take that long? I would have thought that with the way that they look, they'd have gotten it right away."

"They only see what they want to see." Sunny laughed, drawing their attention to her. "You leave her alone, or there will be hell to pay. Just get with your argument and leave the two of us alone while you do whatever it is that you're doing."

"Where is Howard?" She said he had dealt with his personal business and had moved on. "What's that supposed to mean? And don't think that I didn't notice that you've never gotten us anything to eat or drink. What kind of place are you running here if that's the way you treat people?"

"You get what you give." She'd only just learned that, too. If they were mouthy with her, she could give them the same. If they tried to hurt her in any way or form, she could do the same to them. This whole seeing the dead thing was draining at times, but she was getting better at it, and sometimes it was fun. She looked at Sunny then. "I've got an idea that I wanted to run by you about the new women to the family. What if we had lunch with them once a week? It would have to be on the weekend, like a Saturday or something, because Thelma wants to teach starting in the fall, but don't you think it would be fun to get together like that?"

"I've been wanting to do that since I got into this family. Hoping that the men find their mates so that I could have female friends. I've been hanging out with men most of my life or waiting on their sorry asses. When did you want to start?" She said today was as good as any. "Great. I'll contact Rogen and her sisters. Did you know that they've been selected to build the fire station? If you would have asked me, I would have thought it would have been an easy build. A bunch of bricks in a square shape, and poof, you're done. But they're going to make it more appealing to the eyes." They both laughed, and she looked at the dead again. "Do you think they'll get it?"

"I'm thinking that the older Pine has

figured it out. Notice how he keeps looking at the spot in the room nearest the fireplace? That's where his body was when they found it. I think he is remembering that's where he died." She asked her about the other two. "Mr. Pine won't get it until his wife says he can. She's got him so tied up it's like he's not even a person without her influence."

"Howard, they said that the first decision he made had gotten him killed. I'm assuming that his mother was treating him the same way she did her husband." Carrie told her that was about right. "Did he linger, too?"

"No. He came to see me after he was killed. Crying like a baby. He told me that if I could give him a month without his mother around, he'd be all right with being dead. Once I told him that I couldn't do that, he moved on. Poor man. To think that he's been treated the same his whole life and had to resort to killing his family before he could be his own man. Only to end up dead a few hours later." Mrs. Pine stood in front of her. "What is it I can do for you?"

"Howard isn't coming, is he?" She told

her that he was not. "Well, I'll see about that, the little shitter. He wasn't worth the sweat it took me to push him out. Nothing but a pain in my backside. Did you know that he wanted me to allow him to marry and bring some woman into my house? That's not going to happen."

"No, it's not." She looked startled when she so readily agreed with her. "Have you gotten it yet? Why you're here, and Howard isn't?"

"He left me." Carrie agreed that he had. "You'll tell me now or so help me, I'm going to teach you how to respect your elders. Why aren't we able to leave this house?"

"We're dead, that's why." She knew that Mr. Pine senior had gotten it, but it looked to her like he might well have gotten a backbone in dealing with his daughter-in-law, too. "That son of your'n killed us off like we weren't…well, I don't think he meant to kill me. I've been good to him all his life and his little girl, a damn sight better than you've been to him anyways. But I think that me coming into the room the way that I had it what—"

"What do you mean we're dead? Don't you

think I'd notice if I was dead or not? Shut up until I speak to you, you old bastard." Helen looked at her. "We ain't dead if that's the conclusion that you've been waiting on us to get to. I'd know if I was dead or not, and I'm not."

Carrie just stared at the woman. She had a feeling that she figured it out as well that she was as dead as the other two of them were as well. Some people, like this woman, didn't believe they were ever going to die, and it was sad for them, really. Helen marched over to where her body had been found, slumped over the couch like she'd been reaching for something lying just beyond her reach and had died. Well, she had the big axe in the back of her head, which was a testament to how much her son hated her.

"I'm dead, aren't I?" She nodded at the older man. "Thought as much. Can't seem to get it out of my head that I've been killed. You go on now and send me on my way. I'm going to get me a bit of peace and quiet before she comes around and ruins that, too. Damned woman was forever screaming about something not being to her liking. You send me on now, I'm ready.

Hopefully, I can see my missus, too."

Carrie didn't need to do anything to send people on like the elderly man. Once they made peace with the fact that they were no longer living, they just sort of faded out of this plane onto the next. She hoped that he got his time with his missus and had some of the quiet that he'd been craving, too. It had been a real shame that he'd been killed, too. The poor old man.

It didn't take long for Helen to notice that her father-in-law was gone. She bitched at her about doing something with him until she told her to go away. The only thing she could do was wait on them, and once the other man figured it out, he faded away as well. She could only hope that there was a special place for people like Helen.

"I'm not dead." Carrie had had enough and told her that she was. "No. I won't believe it. I've too much to do to be lying around in my casket. You tell that son of mine that he's to come here and do my bidding."

"He's moved on. The same as you should." She said that she refused to believe that he'd do something without her permission. "Yet he did, didn't he?"

Carrie stood up and glared at the other woman. She could see her glancing at where her body had been found. The couch was gone. It had been moved out a few hours after she'd been killed. The only person left, Danielle Pine, Helen's granddaughter, was going to move into the house as soon as she moved here, and hopefully, Helen would have moved on. Or she'd move her on. It made very little difference to her.

"Why are you in charge anyway?" Carrie told Helen that she was and that there was very little that she could do about it. "We'll just see about that, won't we? I want to see your boss. Right now, bring him here."

That made her burst out laughing. And when she told Sunny what she'd said, she laughed too. It took them more than twenty minutes to get their humor calmed down enough to have a conversation with Helen, and by then, she was spitting—literally spitting mad.

"I've had enough." Carrie told Helen that

she was going to send her to the other place if she spit on her once more. Of course, they were never hit by any of the spittle, but it was the fact that she was doing it that pissed them both off. As soon as she could, she was going to banish the woman to the other place — a place that she'd only heard of in order to make it so that she couldn't bother her or anyone else that was in the living area. "You will apologize right now or be gone."

"No, I will not." That was all it took to send her on her way. She had better things to do than sit around and listen to the woman anyway. Snapping her fingers, not only was she gone, but she was also quiet too. It was the nicest thing she could have done for herself. Banishing the woman would be good for a great many people, too, she thought.

By the time she was ready to go out to lunch with the other women, Carrie was in a better mood. All morning, she'd been dealing with the Pine family, and she needed to relax and to chill out. As soon as they were in the restaurant, she did something that she'd never done in her life.

Had a large piece of apple pie before she ate her meal. Of course, the others teased her about it.

"I'm a grown-ass woman who can have pie before her meal. You should try it sometime." The pie was warm with a large scoop of ice cream on it. She moaned at the taste of it. "I mean, I might not even order lunch and have another piece of pie. You guys don't know what it is you're missing."

The others ordered pie, too, and when it was brought to them, she could hear the moans all around the table. Who said you have to eat a meal before you had your dessert had never had a day like she had. Dealing with the living or dead was enough to make anyone upset enough to have a carb-filled luncheon date, too.

She did make herself eat a nice lunch when she ordered. Figuring that the salad would make her feel better after the sugar rush was fun. She didn't even mind that she got a little heartburn from it. But she might well order her another piece for when she was finished. Carrie simply didn't care who stared at her either.

~*~

Danielle looked around the house. It was a great deal bigger than she remembered it being from when she was a child. Of course, she'd never been allowed to be beyond the living room or the kitchen. The dining room was no place for a brat, she'd been told. The first thing she was going to do when she got moved in was have a sloppy meal in the dining room and get food all over the table.

She wouldn't. She knew better than to be a mess anyplace. Her mother and grandmother had been the same type of person as her Grandma Helen had been. Mean. She wasn't sometimes mean either; she was just mean all the time, and she couldn't believe how much she'd hated to come here. Now, it was all hers.

"Ms. Pine, there are a couple of things about the house that you need to be made aware of. Your father lived here until he was killed, so there are things still in his room, as well as the others that called this their homes." She told the attorney that she could deal with it. Mr. Sheppard had been talking to her all along since she'd been notified that her family was all gone.

"Also, while there is enough money in the estate to take care of the matter, there are still a few outstanding bills that will need to be paid."

"You told me that there was money in the estate, correct?" Jameson told her that there was plenty of money, and that was hers as well. "Good. I don't want to sound greedy or anything, but I don't think I could be here without that money. What else should I need to know? I feel like you're holding something back."

"No, I'm not. I swear. But you have been told that your great grandda and your grandparents were killed in the living room, and that is why the couch is missing." She said she'd been told. Danielle turned to him, almost fearful that he'd leave her now that she was here. "It's going to be fine, Danielle. You're going to be just fine."

"Thank you. I didn't know how much I needed to hear that until just now." On impulse, she hugged him. When tears filled her eyes, she didn't release him until she said what she needed to. "You've been kinder to me than any member of my family had been. I wanted to thank you for that."

When she pulled away, he handed her a handkerchief. Danielle hadn't known anyone to carry one of those in all her life. After wiping at her eyes, she told him she'd get it back to him as soon as she could, and he smiled at her.

"You have my number, correct?" Nodding, she told him that she had him on speed dial. "Good. You remember that if you need anything. I'm here for you. I feel…well, I've never had a little sister before, but I'm betting she'd be just like you. I know I keep saying this to you, but you're going to be just fine. I know it."

"Thank you again." She was just ready to grab him again to hug him when someone rang her front doorbell. It was the sound of running elephants, she thought, and she was going to change that as soon as she could. Her grandmother would have done that. She just knew it. Going to the door, she was surprised to see a man standing there with a pizza box and a huge smile. "Can I help you?"

"My brother said you were moving in tonight, and he thought you could use some company for your first meal." When the man entered, she looked at Jameson. He told her it was his brother Archie and his wife, Carrie. Then, before she could close the door, another brother entered, and Nash and Sunny arrived. "Come on honey, where did you want to eat this meal?"

"In the dining room." She thought it fitting, too, that they were going to eat pizza of all things in her grandmother's formal dining room. Never would she allow any pizza in her house, much less in the dining room fit for a queen of the castle. "Oh good, you have soda too. She'd hate every minute of this."

It was by and far the most fun she'd ever had in this house, and she told them so. Archie said that he'd known her grandmother and had never cared for her at all. Even Sunny, who had lived here all her life, had said that she'd never liked the old bitch and often time felt sorry for her son Harold. She felt like they were her friends by the time they left her later that night. Jameson told her once again that she'd be all right. The thing was, when he left her then, she really did feel like she was all right.

Wandering through the house, she found things that she'd noticed as a child and had never been able to touch. Her grandparents' closets were still filled with things that they'd left behind. Jewelry in her jewelry box and powder that she had worn were still there as well. Of course, the bed was made up, a habit that she picked up here when she'd been allowed to visit. There were things like lined-up shoes on the floor in the cupboard. Hats of her grandfathers hanging on the hooks by the door, just waiting for him to return.

The house and its belongings were left to her by her dad, who, since he died last, had gotten it from his parents. There were no taxes to pay up, no mortgage for her to keep up with. Every part of the house was hers so long as she wanted. And if she didn't, then she could sell it and move on with her life. But she wouldn't. It was hers now, and it meant a roof over her head and a place for her to sleep. Something that she'd not had in the last few months of being on her own.

Eight months ago, she'd lost her job and her apartment. Not on the same day, but close enough that she couldn't believe it. The place where she had worked had decided that it didn't want to be open any longer, and the complex that she'd been living in had sold out to a larger company, and they were going to tear the place down.

Jameson was looking into that for her. There should have been something for her to move into when they took her home from her. But no, they'd given them fourteen days to move out, or they'd find their stuff, furniture, and lives stuck in the dumpsters that were on the property the next morning. Luckily for her, she'd been able to sell everything and get out in time. There were families that were in the process of getting out when the big bulldozers came along and crushed their dreams of homelife right into the dirt.

Finding her dad's room in the house wasn't difficult. He'd been raised to keep things nice, and his room showed it. Everything in its place, he'd tell her when she was a child living with her now long gone mother. Debra, her mom, was the exact opposite. Nothing had a place unless it was on the floor.

Some of the things she came across while going through his things brought back memories that hurt her. He'd saved every card that she'd sent him, filing them in a large box marked with her name. There were drawings of hers, too — she'd forgotten that he enjoyed drawing. He'd been good at it too.

His clothing smelled as he did. A little bit of baby powder that he'd put under his arms and the cologne that he would wear on his cheeks. Inhaling deeply, she wondered if she'd miss the scent of him. He'd been out of her life so long that she knew that she'd not miss the man himself. And that she blamed on her grandmother.

Grandma Helen was a terror. She hated her mother and, in turn, hated her too. The handful of times that she'd been to her home had been wroth with fear and anger. She wouldn't allow her to have anything nice in the house because she thought of her as beneath her. Look now, she thought, it's all mine.

Tomorrow, she was going to box up all the clothing and donate it someplace. Then there was the matter of the food and things in the cupboard that she was going to get rid of as well. There had been staff when her family was alive, but Danielle didn't need it. She'd live in her big house and do for herself. If she couldn't get to a couple of the rooms, then no one would know but her, and that's the way she liked it.

Going to bed that night, after stripping off the covers and linens off the big bed, Danielle lay there thinking about her luck. The house she'd been told by Jameson was worth a great deal, in the millions she'd been told, but again, she had no desire to sell it, at least for now. There was a bit of land, too, that she'd been told was bringing in some income, enough to pay the taxes yearly that was rented property. There was also a trust set up by her great-grandda for her too that would ensure that she would have money to keep her in food and beds, he'd said in his will.

He'd been the only person that she'd ever want to be alive if she could. Her father hadn't been around all that much, but her great-grandda had written to her faithfully monthly. He'd been sending her money, too, little bits at a time that would show up just when she needed it. Which was really all the time, but it was nice to have.

Getting up when she knew she wasn't going to sleep, she decided to start her purge in the master suite that had belonged to her grandparents. By the time the sun was coming up, not only had she cleaned out the closets, but she'd been able to box up the items around the room that she'd have no use for. Those things were set aside so that if she decided to have a garage sale, she'd make a bit of cash off those as well.

At noon, she decided to have herself a treat. Walking to the little ice cream shop, she was able to have a shredded chicken sandwich and fries. Never one to like ice cream all that much, she did have a frozen Snickers bar and loved every bit of it. Danielle was just headed back to the house when she saw Jameson and another of his brothers. While she didn't know his name, she knew that they were related for sure.

"I was just coming to see you." Smiling,

she told him how much work she'd gotten done already. "Good for you. Oh, this is my brother Wrangler and his son Wills. They were going to help you out if you need it. Moving full boxes would be too much for you, I think. I saw the size of the boxes you had, and I'm betting that you've filled them to the brim."

"I did, actually. But I was on a roll and thought that if I had any boxes left over, I could divide up the stuff in them. They didn't have much, did they?" Jameson told her that he'd never been in the house until last night with her. "Oh. I thought that you would have been invited, being that you have money. She only associated with people with funds, she told me once."

"It's doubtful I would have come to her home even if invited. She wasn't a person that people wanted to be around." Danielle agreed with him. "Anyway, I was thinking that you could use a hand with the heavy stuff. The three of us can help you out today with whatever you want."

"I was thinking of having a sale, but I don't know how to begin with that. Just putting the things that I don't want out on the sidewalk appeals to me. Then, if no one picks it up, I can have it picked up by someone who deals in this sort of thing. Do you think that would be all right? I don't want to break any rules." Jameson told her that his brother was mayor and that he'd call him to ask. "Thanks so much. I really appreciate that."

Wills made her a 'free' sign once it was established that she could do what she'd had in mind, and even before the second piece of furniture was brought out, people were lined up to take it away. Some of them asked if they could come inside to get the stuff, but Jameson put a stop to that. There was no telling what they'd take in the name of things being free.

By the time dinner rolled around, she was exhausted. Having been up for as long as she had and moving things out, she was ready to call it a day. However, once the women in the leap, she had known that Jameson and his family were shifters, showed up to help clean things, she sat in the living room, now devoid of furniture, and relaxed on her lounger for the yard. She was asleep in no time.

Waking up, not knowing where she was, scared her a bit. But once she realized where she was and what was going on, she found herself in the kitchen where food was being laid out. She'd have to pay Jameson back for this meal as it was Chinese food and pizzas again. Christ, she thought, her body was hurting everywhere for everything that she'd been doing.

"You've got a lovely home here. I'd never been inside, but it's bigger than it looks from the outside, isn't it?" She told Rogen that she'd never been in all the house until yesterday. "I never knew your relatives, but I'd heard about them. Your grannie sounds like a real peach."

"You have no idea. Once, when I was visiting my dad, she made me wear plastic bags on my feet so I'd not bring things into her house. And I wasn't to use the bathroom because I wasn't part of the family that lived there. Great-grandda was a nice man, but he allowed Helen to be the way she was." She asked about her dad. "My dad wasn't all that brave around her. He'd do what she wanted, no matter how much it hurt me in the process. After a while, I just stopped coming around even though he had visitation rights with me. It was just easier to not come here rather than to be treated like pond scum."

"That's so sad." She agreed and was grateful when Weston came over and changed the subject. "I will change the locks as soon as Monday. I've been thinking of other things, too, that I need to worry about. Like the land that I have. Jameson said he'd contact the renters and tell them that I'd get with them soon, but since it's not broken right now — as my grandmother on my mom's side would say, I'm not going to worry about it right now."

There were a lot of things that needed to be taken care of in the house. Not just with the locks, which was important, but there were the outbuildings as well and the things that might be in them. There was a lawn service that came by, as well as someone who cleaned the house once a week that she'd need to decide on if she wanted them to continue or not. She never realized that owning a house could be so thought-consuming. But she'd get to it sooner or later.

Chapter 7

Weston had been studying the blueprints for the new school for the last twenty minutes and still had no idea what he was looking at. Not to mention how many pages there were for him to get equally confused about.

He got that they overlapped for a reason, but for the life of him, he didn't know why there were places on the prints that weren't on the other page. There were whole sections that seemed to be added that had nothing to do with—

"They're upside down, and you start with the last page." He looked up at Sandy when she spoke. "I have a hard time with them as well, but not like someone who's never read them before. Why are you looking at them anyway?"

"I was told I have to approve them." She shook her head and moved them away from him before getting to the first page and putting it in front of him. "This looks great. Is this what I'm hoping to end up with?"

"It is. I'd let someone who knows what they're doing look them over. It's not like you'd know enough to change things, no offense." He told her that there were none taken. "I came here to ask you something. It's about Danny."

"He's still in jail." She nodded and then started pacing the room. "I don't believe that he'll make bond, nor do I think they'll be letting him out for good behavior. He seems to be causing a bit of trouble there, anyway. Also, I think—"

"The house we shared in Tennessee, I'm having it cleaned out. There were several insurance policies there with my name on them. Even a couple with my sister's name on them. I'm...he was going to kill me off too." He waited for her to say more. Sandy knew that she was an immortal, just like the rest of her family. "I was good to him, Weston. Better than I should have been, too. Why would he kill me off?"

"Money. Greed. You know as well as I do that was his motive for killing off Belinda's family. A better question you should be asking yourself is, why did he start with her? I'd want to know why he'd started with the children." She said she'd never thought of that. "To me, it takes a stone-cold killer to kill off children. He seemed to have had no qualms at all about it."

The day before yesterday, they'd had the bodies of Benson and the two children exhumed to see if they were dead before or after the fire started. It had always been assumed that they died in their sleep, overcome with smoke. But now that they knew that Danny had killed them off for the insurance, they were going to dig deeper. To see, he supposed, if he'd killed them all before setting the house on fire.

"I don't understand why it makes a difference. It was all premeditated, right?" Again, he told her that he didn't know, but Jameson would. "To be honest with you, I'm afraid to know what he did. If he killed those two kids with something more than the fire. But then they wouldn't have suffered as much, either. That's what I'm thinking. I know that Belinda has suffered greatly thinking that they would have woken up during the fire and knew that they were going to die. I don't know that I could—what if we'd had children? I know that it's not possible, but—"

"Don't. Just don't do that to yourself. You couldn't have children so there is no point in you thinking about it." She told him that was all she could think about. Would he have killed his own children? "And if I tell you that I think that he would have? That I believe because he had no trouble killing your niece and nephew, he'd have no trouble killing his own? Is that going to make things any less terrible for you?"

"No." She finally sat down, and he could see the tears streaming down her face. Her voice rose as she began to scream at him, but it was what she said that had his heart breaking for her. "I brought him into my family, and they had to pay the ultimate price. He killed my brother and his kids because of me."

Getting up, he went to her and jerked her from the chair. After slapping her, he held her as she broke down. Sliding her back into the chair, he knelt on the floor in front of her while she continued to cry. He didn't want her to think about the things that she did, but he didn't know what else to do with her.

"He would have killed someone else's family, perhaps someone else's entire family. But he didn't. He wasn't able to get to anyone else because of you and your family. You're smart for not allowing him to take over your life, Sandy. You didn't let love color your perception of him. You knew on some level that he had to be watched, and you saved your family. Not alone, but you were there for them when they needed you." She nodded, but he needed for her to say it. "Tell me you understand. Tell me that you know that if not for you and your family, he would have gotten away with not just killing your family but who knows how many others. Tell me that you understand."

"I understand." She held onto him, her grief getting the better of her. "Benson was such a good man and a great father, and Danny killed him because of money."

"You remember that. You had nothing to do with—how was you to know that he was going to be that sort of person? You couldn't have known. None of you could have." She nodded.

"Do you realize how lucky you are? How you keeping tabs on him has saved your entire family. Even when you got here, you never lost sight of him. Coming to one of us when he was out of control. There is no telling what things he might well have done had he been allowed to roam free and not have anyone watching over him."

"He's a monster." Weston nodded, getting up from the floor and sitting in the chair next to her. "You hit me. I'll never forget that, either. You brought me back to my good place by hitting me, and I will forever be thankful for you, Weston. I was…bad thoughts were entering my mind, and I was ready to…I was going to end my life if not for you."

"He's not worth it." She nodded. "And do me a favor. Don't tell your family that I hit you. I think they'd knock me around a bit too."

"I won't. I love you, Weston. You're about the best brother-in-law a girl could have. When she stood up, so did he. After getting another hug from her, he settled behind his desk and asked her if she was all right. "I am. Not entirely. But I know that I will be. I'm headed to the jail. Danny wants to talk to me. Jameson said he'd go with me, and I had declined, but I think I'll call him to take me. I don't want to say the wrong thing. But I do want him to tell me something that can be used against him. Hopefully, there will be a lot of something that can be used against him."

After she left him, he didn't bother picking up the blueprints again. Sandy had been right. He wasn't the person that needed to approve them. Reaching out to Archie, who had dropped off the prints, he told him what Sandy had said about them.

"*I couldn't make heads nor tails out of them either. It wasn't until Carrie suggested that I get someone else to look them over that I thought of you. Why they handed them over to me in the first place is something that I should have asked about. By the way, what are your plans tonight? I have some leap things I have to go over, and I'd like to have your opinion on them.*" He told him that he had plans with his mate. "*Good for you guys. Carrie and I had plans, but this came up. I think I might have bitten off more than I can chew here. It's taking a lot of work to be a leap leader and have a successful business.*"

They talked for a bit more, and he was able to talk his brother into dropping the leap business for now and to go have fun with his mate. The business, he told him, would be there in the morning, but his mate might not be in the mood later. While he wasn't going to take having Danny in the family the way that Sandy did, just knowing that something could come up between mates made him want to spend all the time he could with her. Even being immortal, other things could be coming up that would stall them from being together.

At five o'clock, he was putting the things away that he'd been working on. The blueprints were still on the side of his desk. He'd not bothered with them anymore. He did reach out today to find someone who could look them over. The only person that others told him to ask was his own mate. She'd know right away if the prints were wrong or not.

Sunny, Nash's mate, joined him on his walk home. She told him that she had some news for him and decided that this was the best way to give it to him. Face to face. He wasn't sure if he liked that idea or not.

"There was no smoke in their lungs." He didn't need to ask who she was talking about when she told him that. "They were poisoned and didn't feel a thing with the fire raging around them. I thought perhaps you could tell Rogen, and she'd know the best way to tell her family. It's going to be hard on them either way, but I think Belinda might feel a bit better about them not burning up in a fire. At least I know that I would."

He told her what Sandy had been dealing with. "She had it in her head that it was all her fault that her brother was murdered. I tried to convince her that it could have happened to any family." Sunny said she didn't know if she'd feel any different about him being in the family. "I hope that I helped her at least a little. She was beating herself up over this, and it hurt me."

"She is going to see Danny today, I heard." Weston told her that was where she'd been headed when she left his office. Then he told her that Jameson was going with her. "Good. You know, I can't wait for him to find his mate. The man deserves something special for all the crap he's been through since passing the board. I love the fact that he's going to be helping with the leap, too. He'll be good at that."

"He told me when I talked to him the other day that he was enjoying himself. I didn't tell him that it was because he was new at it. I want him to think he's having fun for as long as he can." Sunny asked him if he was only going to work for the family and for the leap. "I believe so. He's been going over the rules and regulations for the leap for most of his life. He'll know more about them than anyone would by now. Even Archie."

"I know that Archie depends on him a great deal. I do as well for a couple of things that I have going on. He's a good person to have around." Weston agreed. "I have to get home. I have some things going on there that will need my attention that my mom has me looking into. A faerie's life is never dull, I have to admit."

When she left him, he entered his home. It was quiet now. The faeries that lived in his home were off in the gardens with Rogen. As soon as he changed his clothing and joined her in the yard, she asked him what had happened. Telling her what he'd heard from Sunny had her crying too.

"Those poor kids. They were the best, you know?" He said that he wished that he'd met them all. "Benson would have loved you. Hell, he loved everyone. Not so much Danny, but he tolerated him a good deal more than the rest of us did. That's why what happened bothers me so much. Why did he target my brother?"

"This is what I think, and I'm more than likely wrong, but your brother would have been distracted with the kids. I know that Belinda has mentioned to me how much they were into things such as sports and activities. And he was a stay-at-home dad, too. I'm betting that keeping up with those things and Danny being family meant that he wasn't nearly as up on watching him as you guys did." She told him that he could be right. "Did he have a lot of trust with the other man? I mean, would he have been in his home without supervision?"

"If you mean did we have access to each other's homes, then you'd be right in that. I know that I still have a key to Benson's home even though it's no longer there. And it's doubtful to me that Danny ever knocked when he was over. Just go into the house like we did one another." Weston said that he couldn't remember the last time he was at one of his brothers' homes when they weren't there. "Not for us. If we wanted to talk to one of the others, we'd just go into their homes and wait for them. Even going so far as to wash up a few dishes or throw a load of clothes in the washer. We were, at least back then, one big happy family. Or so I thought."

They talked a bit more while she pulled weeds from the garden. There weren't all that many; the faeries had done most of the work, but she'd been outside, and the little people decided to allow her to do some of the work as well. But they would never be that far away if she changed her mind about helping.

By dinner time, she'd called her family to come to the house. They had to know what the meeting was about, yet they all showed up. Sandy looked better than she had when he'd seen her this afternoon, and he was happy about that. He had a feeling, however, that things were about to go from bad to worst. He hated this news for his new family and was going to be there for them all if they needed him to be.

~*~

Danny thought about what Sandy had told him. She'd been snipping at him all the time she'd been visiting him, and he didn't like it. Nor did he care for the fact that she brought herself an attorney. He didn't have one yet, and she was having one like she was the one in trouble.

"There are a few things that I'm going to make you aware of. The first one is that I'm not paying for you an attorney." He'd not even asked her to do that, and she had cut him off before he could say a word. "I'm not going to be paying for a damned thing for you. No matter what you have to say. Also, I'm happy to announce that I've been granted a divorce from you. The judge fast-tracked it for me because of what you've done to my family."

"They were my family, too, you know. And just so you know, I won't acknowledge you divorcing me unless you have to pay me support.

If you had given me children like I wanted, then you'd be paying me more." She said she wasn't doing that either. "Why the hell not? You make enough money to support us both, and I have needs."

"What kind of needs do you have in a jail cell? You don't have a television that I can see, so there are no gaming systems. There isn't a fridge, so no beer of any kind. So, there is nothing that I can think of. Besides, as I said, I'm not giving you shit. You murdered my brother and his kids." He waved her off. "What's that supposed to mean? Did you or did you not kill them for insurance money?"

That was old news. She should have been more forthcoming with some money, and he might not have had to resort to killing them, and he told her that. Although he had to admit that he had enjoyed it. Knowing something that she didn't had been a thrill to him. Then, when the insurance policy had come through, it got him to thinking about killing off the rest of them. It sure was a big payday for him.

He'd only admit this to himself, but he had

hated killing the kids. Besides, they were all right, he supposed. But they were kids. However, in order to make it look like the house just caught on fire, he had to do it. Something that he knew very little about.

Sandy should have given him kids. The more, the better. It would have been fun for him to have one of those food cards so that he could get something from the grocery store anytime he wanted and not have to beg Sandy for money all the time. She also kept harping on him to get a job. Like he was going to do that. He had shit to do, and working a job was going to interfere with that time. His ambition was to be a gamer with lots of followers online.

However, it was the things that she said to him today that pissed him off. Not just the divorce, which was hard enough for him to swallow, but that she hoped he went to prison for the rest of his natural life. And that she'd not think about him once while he was gone. He didn't believe that for a minute. He'd killed off her brother. Surely, she would think of him from time to time. Stupid woman.

Sandy was far from stupid, he knew. She and that damned sister of hers had gotten into construction and had made a big deal of it. They didn't share their good fortune with him, but they'd been about to do so in a different way. Insurance policies.

He'd been able to keep up with the payments, too, when she'd leave her purse just lying around. There were a lot of them that he'd taken out, too. Not just on her family but also on some of the old people around the neighborhood as well. Anyone that was older than dirt was someone that he'd make a bit of money off of.

Then there was that damned attorney. He just knew that the man was a sissy boy, as his daddy used to call queers. There was no way that a man looking that good and wearing suits like he did wasn't a sissy boy. Of course, he thought all men better looking than him was a sissy boy. Not that he thought there were very many good-looking men out there who were better-looking than he was. But this guy was way too nice-looking not to be.

Danny knew that he had shortcomings.

A lot of them. He was only in his late twenties, and he thought and — wait, he was thirty-three... when the hell did that happen? Anyways, he told himself that if anyone asked, he was only going to be in his late twenties. But he was bald as a ball. Christ, it was like he woke up one day, and all his hair was gone. He didn't even have any side hair, either. Just nothing up top of his head to even comb over.

He'd like to think that he made up for it in his dick. But he didn't even do that. One night when Sandy had been mad at him, she'd told him that he had a pencil dick. It had taken him a week of wondering what she'd meant by that to figure out an answer as to what she was calling him. When he did, he hit her for the first time.

After that, he'd hit her anytime she pissed him off. Which was, by his estimations, a great deal. She was forever putting him down, telling him that he was a lazy fuck and that he needed to get out and find himself a job. Also, she told him about them having kids.

"I'm man enough." He still believed that if she'd not cut him off, they'd have a lot of kids running around. Not that he wanted to be responsible for them, but her telling him that he wasn't man enough to impregnate her had made him meaner than a one-dollar bill. Thinking on that, he couldn't remember if he was saying it right or not. But he was mean to her. Then Rogen stepped in.

Christ, he wished all the time he'd started with her dying off. But she was just too clever for him. He couldn't get into her house, where her stuff was hidden away, like her social security number or stuff like that. He didn't even know her birthday. She had kept herself alive by being a mean bitch. Now, here they were in this town and it was like everyone was against him.

He couldn't take a shit without anyone telling on him. He couldn't even sneak in a little drinking while in this little town. Not to mention, there wasn't a bar he could hang out in. The place had four pizza shops and nobody to bring him one when he was in jail either. What kind of podunk town had four pizza shops and not nary a person to deliver things to him?

That got him to thinking about a business

that he could run. If he was out, he'd be lining up people with cars to deliver things to others around town. Not just pizza, though, that's all he'd be using them for, but other things, like groceries and the like.

He could see it now. It'd be called Danny's Drivers, or DD for short. He'd have him a fleet of them, too, just driving around this little town, making people's lives a good deal better because they could get the things that they wanted without having to pay for it. He didn't know how he'd make it work. Just knowing that he had to have cars was hard enough for him to think through, but he could make it work somehow.

Danny knew that he'd never get things that he thought up to work. He was just too lazy. It didn't bother him that he was. In fact, he felt like it was something that a great many people aspired to. Being lazy was a form of working; it was difficult not to do anything all the time and have people do things for you, like his wife. She'd work all day, and if he asked her real nice like, she'd bring him a beer to drink before dinner. Sandy was a sap.

It only just occurred to him that she was indeed a sap. He'd knock her around a bit, get what he wanted, and she'd go off crying to her family. Not that he liked that, but she'd not do a damned thing about it, and that would make him very happy when she'd come around whining again, and he'd backhand her.

She didn't know that he was slightly afraid of her. She was stronger than him and worked out a bit while on the job. Sandy was also a big fucking cat that could rip his throat out without a second thought. Being as smart as he knew her to be, he thought that he was lucky that she'd never unsheathed her claws around him, killing him with just a swipe of them.

Danny had tried once to sell her off to some circus. It turned out that the circus keeper, whatever they called the men who had them, was a shifter himself. And he had threatened to tell on him should he try that stunt again. It was difficult to make any money off of anyone anymore, he thought. Christ, it was like they were all on the same phone service the way they just knew one another's business.

The more he bitched to himself about his wife, the more he wished that he'd killed her off when he'd had the chance. At the beginning of their getting together, it had been a thrill to him, knowing that she had money and worked during the day all day long. It left him to pursue his own fun. However, she was never forthcoming with any cash for him. Not even enough for him to go to the bar and hang out with his fellow lazy men. And there were a lot of them.

"Danny, your attorney is here. Do you want to meet with him?" He asked the man if he had on a fancy suit or a cheap one. "How the hell do I know something like that? You want to meet with him or not? I have better things to do than to figure crap out for you."

"I'll see him." After going to the back of his cell so the door was unlocked, he was free to get out and see the attorney. He didn't know if Sandy had gotten one for him because she felt sorry for him or not, but he wanted to make sure that his outshined hers. It was the least she could do because he was in jail because of her.

Once he was locked to the table and ready

for the attorney, he looked around, wondering if all those cop shows he watched were right in that the mirrors were two-way suckers so they could watch him. He didn't know how he was going to do it, but he was going to test that out. Flipping off the person on the other side, if there was one, he waited to see if they'd come after him or not. Nothing happened, but some old broad came into the room and said she was his court-appointed attorney.

"You're a girl." She told him that she was a woman, actually. "There's been a mistake. I don't want a woman attorney. No offense or anything, but women are just too stupid to be good at attorney works."

"Well, aren't you just a peach? And I wouldn't want you as a client either, though here we are stuck with each other. I've been appointed by the judge, and that's the only person that can break us up. I have a feeling that we're going to be great friends by the end of this." He could hear something off in her voice that said she really didn't believe that, but she was sitting down now, and he didn't like it. "My name is

Suzy Lancaster, and I have some paperwork that you need to sign off on."

By the time he was signing off on the third thing, he'd lost interest in it. She had him signing stuff about her being his attorney, which he didn't like, but like she explained to him, was all there was. But he did perk up when she mentioned insurance.

"You said my wife is suing me on account of me having a life insurance policy on her? That ain't right. I need that in the event something untoward happens to her." He'd heard Lancaster — there was no way he was going to call her Suzy — say untoward a couple of times now and decided he liked it. He was going to use it all the time if he could. "A husband has a right to have insurance on his wife so that when she keels over, he's got himself something to live on."

"She said you'd say that, but she's not going to be making the payments on it anymore. That would make it so that you would have to." Lancaster huffed. "Unless you have some kind of millions lying about to pay these policies off, then they'll be null and void anyway."

By the time he was back in his cell, he'd felt beat up. Not that she ever touched him, but with all the things that she'd been saying to him, his mind felt like it had been wrung out to dry in a storm, and it wasn't feeling too good. All she'd had to have done was just tell him what he was signing instead of her explaining everything to him like he was a simpleton. After a few documents, he just tuned her out. If he was honest with himself, he didn't care so long as he was going to get out of jail soon enough so that he could find Sandy and make her pay for him missing out on opportunities like he was. Damned woman, he was going to have to knock her around a bit too.

Chapter 8

Weston stood in the shower, holding onto the walls as the water sprayed down his body. It had been a hell of a week so far, and it was only Tuesday. Wondering how he was going to be able to do this full-time, he nearly screamed when someone touched him from behind. Turning, he pulled Rogen into his arms and held her.

"I don't know why they'd have you tell the family that he died. It wasn't as if he was related to any of you." He told her what he'd been told from the police station. "Oh. Well, I suppose when you put it like that, I guess it was all right for you to break the news to me, then I tell them. That's the way it happened anyway."

Danny had been in his cell when a water main broke in the ceiling. He'd not been hurt, and there was very little water in his cell at that time. But he'd freaked out when his toilet had been flushed, and the water came up out of it, knocking him back. He'd been killed when he slipped on the wet floor and hit his head on the bed in his cell. It was a terrible accident that was going to cost the city in compensation for his family if they asked for it.

"Danny didn't have any family but Sandy. His parents died when he was just a child, and he had no brothers or sisters." He asked about cousins or anyone. "Not that I'm aware of. As far as I remember, no one showed up at the wedding that they had, and since then, I've never heard of anyone coming around. It's just as well he's gone. I'm assuming that there would have been a long-assed trial for him."

"The feds are handling anything that might come from this accident. I'm going to let them, too. I'm only temporary here, and that's how they want to run it. I'm very all right with them taking that part over." She agreed and laid her head on his chest. "I have a long day today as well. I don't know when I'll be back."

"I understand. I do, as well. We've broken ground for the fire station house, so we're working on getting the ground prepped for the foundation. After that, we have the foundation for the school to prep as well. I don't know how that's going to work. The school and the station are several blocks apart, but we were asked to do it, and I'm going to try my best to get it finished up in time for school next fall."

As they finished up their shower and got dressed, the two of them headed down to breakfast. They'd been working so hard, the two of them, that they were missing each other. Once this thing with the Feds was over and he could get things going on a normal workweek, he was going to take his lovely mate out to dinner and perhaps a nice hotel for the two of them to enjoy a night away from everything going on in their lives.

By the time he got to his offices, Belinda was already there. He loved having her around, and now that she was back to work, too, he had a lot of things for her to do. She'd taken some time off when she'd realized that Danny had indeed killed her family and then how they'd died. He wasn't sure that he'd be able to function again after all that. But she was determined. She told him not to let him get her down. He had to wonder if she'd heard about his death.

"I don't want to talk about it." She'd put up her hand when he tried to explain what had happened to the man in the jail. "I'm going to hope that he suffered slightly before dying, and that will be the end of my thoughts on him. He is nothing to me, and I don't want to talk about him again."

"All right. I can understand that." They got right to work, and by the time lunch rolled around, he was on his way to having the first bit of free time that he'd had since taking over the position of mayor of his little town.

After lunch, he had three calls that he had to make regarding new businesses coming to town. He'd been studying up on the things that he could offer potential businesses and thought that he'd done a good job of selling their town. After the second call, he was called back by the sheet manufacturing company, saying that they'd spoken to their board members and were willing to come to town to look the acreage over where they'd be able to build. He wanted to shout to the world that they were coming, but all he did was act professional and tell them he'd set up the meet and greet as soon as this week.

However, after the call, he did do a little gig in his office while talking to his brothers and mate. This was going to be a big deal soon, and he was happy that he got to be a big part of it. Archie and the others were proud of him, too, they told him. Weston was very proud of himself as well.

It took nearly the rest of the day to set up the meetings that he had for the following day. He supposed he was showing his hand, being this cooperative, but he didn't care. The sooner the building was up and running, the sooner income was coming into the town and the people here. He picked up his phone when it started to ring.

"Acting Mayor Sheppard here, can I help you?" There was a sound like a small intake of breath at the other end, and he waited. When no one answered him, he tried again. "Hello, this is Weston Sheppard, acting mayor. Can I help you?"

"This is George Hathaway. Why are you sending the federal government after me? I no longer live in your town, and I want this harassment to stop right now before I have to sue you." Just as he was about to answer him, Agent Cryer, one of the men who had been working with him, came into his office, followed by Belinda. "I'm on vacation, and you having me arrested — or attempting to is messing with my time. Didn't my son tell you to stop looking into my life? I have things just about where I want them."

The agent handed him a note and said to ask the man. After asking Hathaway where the rest of the money was, the man shrieked at him, telling him that he'd gotten it fair and square. That he wasn't to worry about that again. He was told to put it on speakerphone and to try to keep the man on the line for as long as he could. Taking his cues from the agent, he asked him where the money was again.

"I have it in good hands. My wife and I didn't make enough money for that job, and I deserved a bigger cut. Do you have any idea how…well, perhaps you do. Knowing how hard the job is, you'd have to understand what I was doing in order to see that I worked very hard for the money I have now. You're not getting it back." He was told to ask why he called him. "To have you stop sending the feds after me. Damn it, man, they're looking for me everywhere, and I'm running out of patience with you in sending them after me. I'm not going to give up the money, and that's all there is to it. Find it someplace else. That's what I had to do to get some."

"You stole it from the town." Hathaway asked him why he'd care he was just a temp in the whole mess. "Because I'd like for this town to be here in twenty years. The money that you stole from here was to go for a new school, a new fire station, and for the new jail. Because of you, a man was killed when the water main that you knew about burst and killed someone."

"You are not going to blame that on me. I don't care about that little town in only that it gave me enough money that I could retire on. And then you come around having the feds coming after me every time I turn around.

I've had to move twice because of you and I don't plan on it again. I like it right well in the Bahamas." Weston looked at Cryer, and he winked at him. "Now you listen here, young man, I've had about enough of your bothering me. You just do whatever you need to do to keep them off my back, and I'll send you a bit of cash. It won't be enough for you to live the high life, but it will give you a start on understanding why I'm not there anymore. Little towns are the best for robbery."

"Did you just admit to me that you knew you were robbing the town of its taxes and other funds?" Hathaway laughed and said it wasn't like the feds were ever going to find him. So yeah, he was admitting to it. "You're a fool. And a thief. I hope they catch you wherever you are and throw the book at you, you slimy piece of shit."

While Hathaway kept bragging about his ill-gotten gains, Cryer stepped out of the office and pulled out his cell phone. He couldn't hear what was going on at the other end of the call. He heard the man tell whomever he was talking to that their man was in the Bahamas and had given them coordinates to find him. Weston hoped that he was talking to the man when they found him.

"You know what, I remember you now, you little pisser. You and your brothers were children of that bitch of a mother of yours. I remember her beating the shit out of you whenever you were out of her sight. Yes, now there was a good citizen. I believe it was her, too, who told me that I needed to make sure that the jail was taken care of so that she could — didn't she get herself killed in the jail? Something to do with you boys of hers?" He laughed, and Weston listened to him talking about his mother. "Yes, that was it. Wasn't it? She got herself killed by something going on at the jail. Oh, what a woman she was, that one. I think you're well and good rid of her. She certainly knew how to keep me in order."

A few minutes later, the line was disconnected, and he hung up the phone. Looking at Cryer and knowing the look on his face was a good one, he had to laugh. He'd bet anything that the fugitives in the Bahamas were well and truly caught. He just wished he'd been able to see the look on Hathway's face when they showed up at his door while still on the phone with him.

"It's still going to be a while for the money to come back to the town." He told him that he'd figured no less. "I'll be able to get you some money on helping out that will come to you personally that you can get. You were instrumental in getting them arrested."

"Will they come back here to serve out any jail time?" He didn't so much as blink. "I see. I don't really, but I guess I can understand why they'd not be here. It would be a big deal to the town to have them in jail here, I'm betting."

"We'll keep you in the loop on what we can, Mr. Sheppard. But you have to realize that there is a great deal that we can't tell you." He told him that he understood. "Thank you for that. And as I said, there is a reward amount coming to you for your help in their capture. I only hope that it is enough to make you know what a great help you have been."

He didn't know how much of a help he'd

been. The man had called him. He had a feeling that Belinda had called the agent and alerted him to the call, but she only told him that he was caught, and that was all that mattered. Weston decided that he'd give her the money, no matter what it was, because of all the people he knew, she deserved it more than most.

The rest of the day was spent on going over contracts with Jameson. He said he was getting good at them and could spot trouble right away. He hoped that his little brother would be able to open his own offices soon. He deserved it, too.

By the time he was ready for home, having spoken to Rogen several times throughout the day, he was exhausted again. The day had ended on a good note, the money had been transferred to his account just over an hour later, and he, in turn, transferred it to Belinda's account. It was just under five hundred thousand dollars, and she cried when she realized what he'd done. While Belinda wasn't really his sister-in-law like Sandy was, he still loved her as if she were one. She had been through a great deal, and he wanted her to be happy.

Rogen wasn't home when he got there. She was still on the job site, working on one of the things going on around town. Gathering up what he'd need to go and see her, he had packed up a picnic dinner for the two of them. He was pulling into the lot just as the equipment was being turned off.

"I thought we'd have us a little us time." Rogen was all for it and told him she knew just the place they could dine. As soon as they were in the little tree grouping, he thought of all the things that he wanted to do to his lovely mate. But she was falling asleep on his watch, and it was all he could do to get her to eat dinner. She'd been working much too hard, and he needed to do something about it.

After making a few calls, he was able to get Sandy to cover for her sister the next day. Taking her home, Rogen kept telling him that she was all right when he knew better. He didn't think she was sick or anything; she was just exhausted. As soon as he got her home, telling her that she had the entire next day off, she went to bed and closed her eyes. Weston watched over her as she slept.

~*~

Rogen felt better than she had in a while. Rolling out of bed, she took a quick shower and decided that since it was her that messed up the picnic yesterday evening, she'd go see Weston in his office and break a few pieces of furniture while playing around with him. Almost as soon as she closed the door to his office—telling Belinda to go away, she sat on his desk with the food and fed him grapes while telling him what she was going to do to him.

"First things first, I'm going to feed you so that you have plenty of strength to fuck me." He took the grapes from her and nearly choked, trying to get them in his mouth. "You idiot. Don't kill yourself. We have the rest of the day to have some fun."

"What kind of fun did you want to have? I'm all for it no matter what." She told him that she wanted him right there on his desk. "My pleasure. I just have a few things to move here so that we don't break them. Then I plan on breaking you."

Putting his laptop on the floor, he moved the picnic basket to be beside it. As his movements were slow, she could feel her pussy getting wetter by the moment. When he put his hand on her legs, she was so glad she'd worn a dress. It made things much easier for the two of them. Then he planted her feet onto the arms of his chair. As he held them there, stroking the inside of her ankle, all she could think about was him having her. Any way that he wanted.

Weston moved his hands up under her skirt slowly to her thighs, and then he pulled her panties off. She knew that he could smell her. She could smell herself. That spike of need was taking her breath away. It was all she could do not to pull him to her and have him eat her. When he asked her to lie back on the desk, Rogen did as he asked and waited. She didn't have long to wait as he buried his mouth over her and suckled at her pussy, bringing her up off the desk quickly, only to be pushed back down by his gentle hands.

The climax took her breath away. It had hit her hard and consumed her. Even as Weston fucked her with his tongue, she held onto the sides of the desk and enjoyed herself. Christ, he was good at this, and she didn't want it to ever end.

She came so many times, from hard climaxes that took her breath away to small, short releases that seemed to come from the bottom of her feet to her head. She was left feeling like she couldn't go on to wanting more from him so that she could hit the epic climax that would render her unconscious. Rogen wanted it all.

Putting her legs up and over his shoulders, Rogen rode his mouth, using her hips and legs to do so. His tongue was doing all kinds of things to her pussy, fucking her and licking her from gate to clit that she came so many times that she didn't know if she'd survive. Weston slid one of his fingers into her pussy, and she nearly came up off the desk. Grabbing a handful of his hair, she pressed him tighter against her and begged him for more.

Rogen was limp with her releases and didn't know if she could handle even one more. She could barely move when Weston stood up.

She thought for sure that he was finished with her, so she tried to sit up to touch him. Instead, he worked his pants open and teased her pussy with his cock. It was too much, and she begged him to stop. But all he did was slam his cock deep within her.

She came screaming his name. Reaching up to hold onto him, she was delighted when he leaned over her and took her mouth. She could taste herself on his lips, and it was delicious. Even as he fucked her, slowly like he was trying to torture her, she knew that deep in her heart that when she came with him, she was going to come apart, holding onto the only man that she would ever love.

He abused her breasts, her nipples, and throat with his mouth. As he suckled at her breasts, he nibbled too at her nipples, making them hard and painfully full feeling. Rogen wanted more from him, everything that he could give her, and she knew that if asked, he would give her the moon.

Wrapping her legs around his waist, he filled her more. Tightening her pussy around him, she heard his moan of pleasure. Just as she was starting to feel like her body was readying for a release, she held onto him. As he fucked her harder, quicker, with each stroke feeling like it was hitting her in the back of the throat, her body readied for what was to come. When he stiffened and threw back his head, she marveled at the sight of him coming as he growled deep in his body. Christ, she nearly forgot to come watching him in all his glory. When she came then, her body bowing back on the desk, Rogen blacked out just as Weston was telling her that he was coming again.

When she woke, she was on his lap, his cock still deep inside of her while he held her. He was breathing hard, as hard as she was, and it was wonderful. Tightening her arms around him, he kissed her on the mouth and asked her if she was all right.

"I'm not sure." He laughed a little and said he was feeling the same way, like the rug had been pulled out from under him, and he'd had the most delightful time. "I feel like I've been turned inside out. Then turned the other way until it just wore me out."

"I'm feeling like that too. I love you, Rogen Sheppard." She kissed him, a quick kiss on the mouth as he held her. "I hope you brought food with you. I skipped lunch today to do some banking, and I could eat a horse."

They dined on the food that she'd brought. It wasn't nearly enough, so they ordered takeout and had it delivered to their home. On the way there, walking as she had to come and see him, she told him how her day had begun, and he told her about the check he'd had transferred to Belinda. She thought that she'd cry. She'd married such a wonderful person in Weston. And she couldn't believe that she'd not wanted anything to do with him at the beginning.

The food arrived just as they were getting out of the hot tub. Having it delivered at six when they wanted it had been perfect. Her body wasn't nearly as sore as she'd been walking home, but she was happy, too. The tub had done them both a great deal of good. Now, all they had to do was eat and enjoy the rest of the evening together. It was just the way she thought couples did an early night of debauchery.

After eating their dinner, the two of them sat on the couch and read the newspaper. It didn't take all that long, there were only about four pages of it, and most of it had to do with the sports around town. She found herself dozing off just as the clock was chiming for nine o'clock, and she was ready for bed. Getting a good night's sleep was paramount after spending some good fucking time in his office. She might have to take him in his dinner more often if she felt like this at the end of the day.

Laughing, she made her way to bed with Weston. They both had plenty to do and to take care of, but she thought that she could stand it better if they were to take time for each other instead of catching little bits of time when they could manage it. The evening had been perfect, and she couldn't have been more happier if she'd been able to spend a week in bed with Weston. This is what she had wanted all along. To be loved and taken care of by the man that she loved.

At midnight, she heard the phone ringing.

It wasn't any ring that she knew, so she let it go. Getting up to go to the bathroom, she did look to see who it was and noticed that it was an unknown number. Putting the phone back on the stand, she did her business and headed back to bed. Just as she was lying down, it rang again. Picking it up, she decided that at one in the morning, she didn't need to be nice.

"You'd better have a good reason for calling me at this hour. If not, then I'm going to hunt you down and—" The caller said she was her mother. "My mother is gone. Thanks for bringing that up. She died about ten years ago now."

"I didn't actually die but was in a coma. Your father told them to tell you that." She didn't know whether or not to believe her. Then she started spouting off things that only she would know. Or someone that had done a good background check on her. "Do you believe me now?"

"No. I don't know who this is, but surely you could have called at a better hour than one in the morning." She told her that she'd only just arrived in town. "Good for you. If you are my mother, which I still don't believe that you are, you know that I'm a very hard-working person who needs to be in bed by ten to get up at an ungodly hour to work. Who is this really?"

"My name is Glenda Watson. I've been looking for you and your brothers and sister for the last three months. If not for the advertisement in the paper, I might well still be looking." Lying down, snuggling next to Weston as he asked her who it was, she told him that someone saying she was her mother was calling. He, too, couldn't believe it was now that she decided to call. "What will it take for you to believe that I'm your mother? I don't know what else to tell you."

"Call back tomorrow at a decent hour. I'm not saying that I'll believe you anymore, but I know that right now, I'm pissed off because of the time and the fact that you were supposed to have died nearly five years ago. Where is Dad in all this? I heard, too, that he's gone to another country just to deal with his grief. Nothing you can say will change my mind at this hour. Call back tomorrow."

Hanging up on her mom gave her a satisfaction that she'd never felt before. Rogen had never gotten along with her mom, her father, either for that matter, but telling her that she was still alive when she'd gone to her funeral with the rest of her family just wasn't cutting it. Awake now, she got out of bed and made her way downstairs to look on the computer about her mother's death.

She'd been in a car accident while driving drunk. It would have taken a great deal of alcohol to get her mom drunk as she was a shifter, too, but at the time, neither she nor any of the others had thought about that. Their mother had been drinking since they were born and didn't really think about how much it would take for her to be drunk enough to have an accident and die. It just didn't make any sense as to why she'd come around now.

If she remembered correctly, it had been Calhoun who had notified them of her death. She thought about waking him up to see what he had to say, but just as she was convincing herself that this was all a scam for some reason, her brother called her.

"I just heard from someone telling me that she was our mom." She told him that she'd gotten the same call just a little while ago. "I hung up on her. I don't know what sort of scam this is, but I'm not playing with her. Mom died, and the insurance policies that we had paid off. We went to the funeral and had a party in her honor. Who is this person that is trying to cause trouble?"

"Did you actually tell her that we had a party in her honor?" He said that he'd not but wished that he had. "Why couldn't any of this have waited until a decent hour? She told me that she just got into town, and I no more believe that than I do she's our mom. What do you suppose is going on right now?"

"Hang on, I'm getting a call from Toby. He's going to be pissed." When she hung up the phone, she reached out to her family to get things settled up about this. If this person really was their mother, why the fuck didn't she reach out to them all instead of using a phone. And how did she get her phone number? There were more questions than answers about this, and she wanted to hunt her down and figure this out. *"She said that she was in a coma for the last few years and that Dad lied to us."*

They had each heard from her by now, and the only one who hadn't had been Belinda. If the person really was her mother, then she'd missed out on a lot of things. Like the death of Benson and the grandchildren, Belinda moving to Ohio to start a new life, and even Toby's kids, all of them under the age of seven.

"I was just thinking about contacting Dad. It's been a while, but I should be able to talk to him." Calhoun said he'd do it now. *"All right. I know that we should more than likely wait until later in the morning, but whatever this woman is up to, it's not going to go over well with anyone if she's lying."*

Calhoun didn't contact their dad with all of them on the same link. She thought that was smart of him. If she was indeed alive, then he'd be the one to get pissed off at their father rather than all of them at one time. If she was really alive, she was going to be really pissed off at both of them. There just wasn't any reason for them to be told that she was dead when she had been kicking around for some time now. At least the three months she'd told her that she was looking for them. And that, too, bothered her. Why didn't she reach out? Why do this on the phone? No reason that she could think of other than she wasn't really their mother.

Weston joined her in the office and brought her a cup of tea and some of the cookies that had been in their picnic dinner tonight. She was just munching on them when her brother contacted her again. The news wasn't good.

"Whoever she is, she's not our mother."

Before You Go...

HELP AN AUTHOR

write a review

THANK YOU!

Share your voice and help guide other readers to these wonderful books. Even if it's only a line or two, your reviews help readers discover the author's books so they can continue creating stories that you'll love. Log in to your favorite retailer and leave a review. Thank you.

AWARD WINNING, BESTSELLING AUTHOR

Kathi Barton, a winner of the Pinnacle Book Achievement Award and a best-selling author on Amazon and All Romance books, lives in Nashport, Ohio, with her husband, Paul. When not creating new worlds and romance, Kathi and her husband enjoy camping and going to auctions. She can also be seen at county fairs with her husband, an artist and potter.

Her muse, a cross between Jimmy Stewart and Hugh Jackman, brings her stories to life for her readers in a way that has them coming back time and again for more. Her favorite genre is paranormal romance, with a great deal of spice. You can visit Kathi online and drop her an email if you'd like. She loves hearing from her fans. aaronskiss@gmail.com.

Follow Kathi on her blog: http://kathisbartonauthor.blogspot.com/